WITCH HEIST IN WESTERHAM

Paranormal Investigation Bureau Book 11

DIONNE LISTER

ISBN 978-1-922407-00-9

Paperback edition

Cover art by Robert Baird

Content Editing by Hot Tree Editing

Line edits by Chryse Wymer

Proofreading Hot Tree Editing

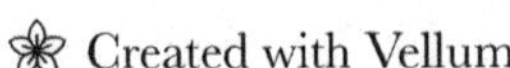

CHAPTER 1

Well, this was eye-opening. The model strutting down the catwalk to the strains of Harry Styles's "Adore You" wore a sequined green top with spaghetti straps and the plungiest neckline I'd ever seen. The top skimmed the inside of her boobs, stopping just before each nipple. I'd never have the guts to wear something like that… not that I could afford the designer price tag. Although, maybe if I looked like a model, I would've been game to wear it. Actually, maybe not.

As she passed us and neared the end of the platform, her skyscraper heel caught on something. She jerked forward and hopped as she tripped. I sucked in a breath. She scrambled to stay on her feet. Was she or wasn't she going to…? Phew! She managed to save herself, turn, and make her way back along the catwalk. She hadn't even looked down to check herself, and she really should have. I mean, wasn't there a breeze where there shouldn't have been? The top, which had only just covered things, had shifted, revealing both nipples.

Will's eyes were wide open. When he'd agreed to come to the London fashion show to see his sister working, I bet he hadn't imagined he'd get such an eyeful. He probably wasn't disappointed though. I turned my head and looked at Beren. He didn't appear to be overly disappointed either. We couldn't blame them, but Liv and I still shared a head shake. At least it hadn't been Sarah, Will's sister, who'd flashed the world. I couldn't imagine what Will would've done then since we weren't allowed to use our magic in public.

"It's Sarah," Will said. I looked at the catwalk. It was the first time I'd ever seen her at work. I already knew she was gorgeous, but wow. Her five-feet-nine frame was made way taller by nude platform heels. She wore a red mid-thigh-length dress with a low neckline, but not as revealing as the previous model's. Her sheer sleeves were fluted at the ends, the fabric slightly longer than her hemline. She gave us a flirty smile as she strutted past. I sighed. Models with their long limbs did everything so nicely and elegantly. It was as if they were from another planet. I knew I should be happy with myself because there was nothing wrong with how I looked, and my body worked just fine, but I sighed. It would be nice to feel stunning for five minutes, be the one everyone oohed and aahed at when I entered a room. Oh well, no one could have everything. Time to get over it.

Two more models walked by, and as the last one made it to the end of the runway, the lights went out. Totally black. That was brave of the designers. What if one of their models fell off the stage?

The music continued playing. Well, this was weird. Was it a statement from the designer? Yeah, nah. As if they'd go to those lengths to make things dramatic. Although, people had probably tried weirder things to sell stuff.

The music stopped. A woman's voice came over the microphone, her posh English accent calm, as if nothing untoward was unfolding. "I'm very sorry about this, everyone. If you could stay seated, we'll get this sorted in a jiffy."

Phone torches lit up around us, people unable to bear more than a minute without illumination. Some of them were texting or maybe posting on social media. I supposed if you were rich and always flitting from fashion show to party to fashion show, not much bad stuff happened. This was probably a really negative experience for them. I chuckled.

There were a few murmured conversations, but the dark seemed to muffle people's desire to talk loudly. Will whispered, "What's so funny?"

"I'll tell you later."

"Ah-huh." The tone in his comment meant he got me. And that, folks, was why we were still together. We understood each other. I smiled. Affection and love filled my chest. His hand felt for mine, and we entwined our fingers.

During the fashion show, I'd been getting pings of magic from many different people—there were obviously a few witches working in the industry—but a strong spike of magic elbowed me in the back of the head. I rubbed my scalp. That had never happened before. Had I become even more sensitive to magic? Just what I needed—something else that could give me a headache.

The crowd's murmuring grew louder, and a couple of people complained, threatening to leave. The lights flickered and came back on. The two people who were going to leave sat back down.

A shrill scream came from backstage. Will and Beren jumped up and picked their way through the two rows in front of us, then ran to the backstage area. Once an agent, always an agent.

"Is this part of the show?" came from the row in front of us.

"I don't know," a woman answered, "but they do look like models, so maybe?" I had to agree—Beren and Will radiated gorgeousness. Liv and I were lucky girls because they weren't just good-looking; they were both wonderful humans.

I turned to Liv and leaned over Beren's chair towards her so I could talk quietly. "Hey, should we go and see what's up? Maybe they need our help."

She looked around, then back at me. "Um, I can't really do anything. Maybe you should go check. Text me if you're not coming back."

A tall, slim man in a spiffy white suit came through the curtains and onto the stage. He held a microphone. He walked to the middle of the catwalk and peered around the room until everyone was quiet. "Our apologies, but we have to cut this evening short. If you could make your way to the foyer, we'll be serving complimentary champagne and canapés. Again, our apologies, and thank you for coming tonight to Evelyn's show. We hope you like what you've seen. Good evening."

Well, there went me going to see if they needed help. I slid my phone from my bag and texted Will. *Is everything okay? Will you be long?*

Not sure how long we'll be. Something's happened. Take Liv and go downstairs.

Is everyone okay?

I don't have time to fill you in. Please just go downstairs. We'll be there as soon as we can. I hmphed. I hated not knowing.

I eyed the door to backstage, wanting so badly to go through it.

My phone vibrated with another message. *Don't even think about it.* My mouth dropped open. How did he know? I sighed. Okay, so he knew me too well.

I hmphed. *Okay, fine.*

I told Liv the situation. "Do you think someone died?" she asked.

"I have no idea." I glanced at the backstage curtains and the door next to the stage again. Tempting as it was, I'd been given instructions, and I wasn't in the mood to get into trouble. "He said they'll be down soon enough. Come on." Behaving wasn't nearly as much fun as it should be—if it was, people would do it way more often, and by *people*, I meant me.

Liv and I waited till the *beautiful* crowd had left in a smog of allergy-inducing perfume before we made our way out and down the stairs to the ground floor. In the spacious reception area, waitstaff in black-and-white livery served alcohol and expensive-looking finger food from silver trays. We stood to the side—all these Botoxed, expensively dressed people were intimidating. I was just a normal person, and I was sure they could tell. Maybe I needed to get out of my own head. If they looked down on me, who cared? Besides, I could do magic, and most of them couldn't. Come to think of it, I could buy nice fabric and magic my own designer clothes into being if I was really that worried about it. To be honest, I couldn't be bothered. There was my answer. I laughed to myself.

"What's so funny?" Liv popped an hors d'oeuvre in her mouth.

I grabbed one off the proffered tray. "Just realising how silly I am. Nothing new." I laughed.

"Well, fair enough, then." She smiled. "I wish I knew what was going on up there. What if it's dangerous?"

"I can't feel anything *unusual.* Besides, if it were dangerous, Will would have told me to get you out of here ASAP."

"True."

An older woman, her white hair slicked back and her ears glittering with what I assumed were diamond earrings, abruptly stopped talking. She slapped her hand on her mouth, her eyes wide. She frantically jerked around, then hurried away but didn't make it more than ten feet before she threw up all over the floor. *Splat*! *Splat*! Splashes from the impact with the timber floors flung up and soiled a man's black trousers. I cringed and put my own hand over my mouth.

Ew.

A man rushed over to help her. Across the room, another young man hurled, in sympathy, down the front of his companion's green dress. A large chunk hit her mouth. Oh, God. The wearer of said dress, a red-haired young woman, opened her eyes wide, then returned the favour by vomiting on his shirt. Hands over our mouths, Liv and I watched in horror as the domino effect continued. Oh, God, three more people evacuated their finger food and drink, plus probably what they'd had for lunch earlier, onto the floor and, disgustingly, onto the people around them.

I pinched my nose against the putrid odour, or I would soon follow. Was this just a room full of weak-stomached people, or was the food contaminated? I grabbed Liv's arm and dragged her to the entry vestibule and out the automatic front doors. No good could come from staying there, and I didn't want to be the next domino to fall.

Once we were in the cold but fresh air, I let my hand fall from my face. "How much did you have to eat?" I asked Liv.

"One hors d'oeuvre. What about you?"

"One." We stared at each other, waiting for any telltale

signs of impending stomach-related doom as the London traffic zoomed past. "Maybe there was one bad batch, and we were lucky enough to have avoided it?"

"I don't want to speak too soon, but I think you might be right."

My phone rang. Will. "Lily, we're going to be up here a bit longer. Can you come up and sit with Sarah?"

"That doesn't sound good."

"It's not. Just go back up the stairs and go through the door I went through earlier."

"Okay. See you in a minute."

Liv stared at me. "What happened?"

"I'm not sure. He wants us to go up and sit with Sarah." Sarah was in town for a few days after the show and was staying with us so we could make the most of the time she had here.

"Well, let's go."

We covered our mouths and noses as we entered the vomitorium, and I wasn't talking about the ones at the Roman amphitheatre. Sirens wailed from the street—ambulances must've been called. I pitied those paramedics and hoped they had face masks.

I ran to the stairs and avoided staring at the carnage, Liv right behind me. The groans and calls for more buckets and mops were enough to churn my stomach. I took the stairs two at a time. Who needed to be elegant? Not me.

We hurried back into the room with the stage. I threaded my way through the chairs and jogged to the closed door. The calm of the stage area did not prepare me for what was on the other side.

As soon as I opened the door, a tidal wave of animated

chattering and crying broke over me. Models, designers, and make-up artists crowded the room.

"Where's the patient?" I swung around. Two paramedics stood there. A young, petite blonde woman carried a bag. "I said, where's the patient?" Her grim expression spoke of a need to get there quickly.

I shook my head. "I'm sorry. I don't know. I only just got here. I'd say through there." I stared at the throng of people.

The blonde woman and her middle-aged male colleague walked purposefully into the crowd. I wrinkled my brow. "Will didn't say someone was badly hurt. Maybe they tripped in the dark?"

Liv shrugged. "Your guess is as good as mine."

Another duo in paramedics gear came in, as did four police officers. Before they could ask, I said, "That way."

"Thanks," a tall guy about my age said before he and his colleague headed off to push through the gorgeous mass of models and support staff. Some of them craned their necks to see above others to whatever was happening on the far side of the room. Others animatedly waved their hands and frowned as they talked among themselves.

"How the hell are we going to get through that mess?" I asked Liv.

"Maybe text Will, ask him to send Sarah over here."

"Oh, great idea. I'm not too bright sometimes." I texted him.

He replied quickly. *Sarah's just being seen by the paramedics. She should be okay to go soon.* My mouth dropped open. I read the message out to Liv, then looked up at her. "Surely he could have mentioned that titbit before? Seriously? And how okay is okay?"

Liv lowered her voice, although it was probably unnecessary because there was so much other noise, no one would've heard her. "Beren could have healed her, surely."

Hmm. "Maybe if she was hurt in a crime, they wanted to have a record of her injuries."

"True." She bit her bottom lip. "So now what?"

"I guess we wait." I glanced around and spotted a few chairs next to a table. A plethora of make-up sat in what looked like a tackle box on it. We took two chairs and waited and waited. Two more teams of paramedics hurried through. What the hell had happened? My other question was, why did Will call us up here if Sarah wasn't ready? I would've been concerned for her health except Beren was here, and there was no way Will would have let her wait for healing if it were life-threatening. Eventually the crowd parted, and she stepped through, Will and Beren at her side.

She'd dressed in an emerald-green jumper and blue jeans. A bandage swathed her head. Crap. I jumped up and met them halfway. "Oh my God. What happened?"

Beren stopped. "Hang on a sec, Lily." He turned to Sarah and indicated the chairs Liv and I had been sitting on. "Sit there for a moment, and I'll *you know what.*"

She nodded, winced, and groaned. "That was a bad move." She slowly walked with Will's help and sat. Beren bent slightly and gently placed his hands on either side of her head. His magic warmed my scalp for a couple of minutes, then ceased as he dropped his hands.

He smiled. "How does that feel?"

She sat still, then nodded and shook her head, testing herself. "All good. Thanks, B. You're the best."

Beren grinned. "Yeah, I know." Liv and I rolled our eyes. "Anyway, we'll leave the bandage on for now. Don't want anyone wondering about your speedy recovery."

Liv chuckled. "Don't give him fodder, please, Sarah. I have to live with his big head."

Sarah stood. "Oops, sorry. I should know better. If he's anything like my brother...." She smirked at Will but quickly dropped it.

"Hey, you gotta call it like it is sometimes, and B and I are both awesome. There's no denying it."

I looked at Sarah. "What's wrong?"

She blinked, her eyes glistening. Were those tears? "One of my good friends has gone missing. In all the kerfuffle, she's just... gone." She opened her mouth to say more, but paramedics wheeled a woman on a stretcher past. She looked to be about forty-five and had an unremarkable face. Definitely not a model. After they passed, another stretcher came through with a model—the blonde one who'd worn a low-cut green pants suit that screamed 70s throwback. A bandage also cocooned her skull. She gave a limp wave to Sarah on the way through.

"Still looking fabulous, Olga," Sarah said, forcing a smile. I knew her well enough to see through her attempt at happiness.

She gave a wan smile. Her Russian accent was thick. "Thank you, darling." And then they wheeled her through the door, and she was gone.

"I thought B and I would have to stay, but we've got what we need. Let's leave," Will said. "There's more to this, and I need to update Ma'am. Come on." Hmm, of course there was. When wasn't there? I used my other sight to check out who were witches and who weren't. Only a couple of the models were, and four other people, including one of the police officers. Interesting. I knew some witches became police, but I hadn't come across any until now. I guessed someone had to tell the PIB when they thought magic had been used in a crime, although we did have our sworn-to-secrecy non-witch allies.

We turned towards the door when a sultry, mature female voice came from behind us. "Wait up, lovelies." She was a regular non-witch. Although there wasn't actually anything regular about her, except for her lack of magic ability. She'd had fillers and probably Botox, and who knew what else, because I couldn't tell how old she was. Was she thirty-five or sixty-five? The only thing that gave away her age was the wrinkly neck. She had massive fake eyelashes, hot-pink eyeshadow, and a tall—made taller by five-inch platforms—skinny physique, which she'd clothed in skintight silver sequined jeans and a hot-pink long-sleeved top with angel sleeves, like the one Sarah had worn during the show. "Where are you going with my favourite model?"

Will edged to the front of our group and held his hand out. "I'm Will, Sarah's brother. Lovely to meet you…"

"Evelyn Taylor. I'm the designer. Pleased to meet you, Will." She shook his hand and fluttered her lashes. She would have coyly looked up at him, but she was too tall for that, and with those shoes, taller than him. I pegged her for a former model. Her graceful movements were obvious, even through the flamboyance. "How is it that you're not working alongside your sister? I could use a man like you… in my shows." She gave him the once-over. I narrowed my eyes, but not wanting to embarrass Sarah, I did my best to open them again, resulting in a weird two-eye twitch. Liv stared at me, alarm evident in the widening of her eyes. Her headshake was so subtle, I almost missed it.

Will gave the woman his most gorgeous smile, his dimples taking centre stage. "I'll leave the modelling to Sarah. I wouldn't want to show her up." He winked.

Evelyn giggled, and despite my best intentions, I rolled my eyes. Okay, so I didn't have any intentions to stop myself whatsoever. Liv pressed her lips together, trying not to smile. Evelyn turned to Sarah. "Seriously, gorgeous, I want to know you're okay. You've had a terrible knock to the head. Are you sure you'll be all right?"

Sarah nodded and winced. Impressive acting there. "I have Will and his girlfriend, Lily, to look after me. I'll be fine." She glanced at me, then Will. "I haven't seen them for weeks and weeks. I've been looking forward to catching up with them, actually." How nice of her to throw that bit in there.

Evelyn gave me a side-eyed glance before smirking, thereby dismissing me as no competition. "All right, but let me know if you need anything. Are you going to be okay for the Swiss show the week after next? I'm down two models now." She pouted.

"I'll be fine. Promise."

Evelyn held out her arms. Sarah stepped into them for a quick hug. They both air-kissed each other's cheeks and stepped back. Evelyn gave a cutesy finger wave to Will as we turned and left. Lucky for me he wasn't a model travelling the world with a group of gorgeous women. I would've missed out nabbing him. Who'd want a normal woman when you could have one who looked like a goddess? Gah, being insecure was hard work.

Will made a show of helping Sarah down the stairs. On the ground floor, a team of mask-wearing cleaning staff was trying to get vomitgeddon under control. Shame they couldn't just hose the whole thing down. The stench was gag-inducing, and I did my best not to add to the carnage as my dinner edged up my throat. I wasn't the only one who slammed a hand over their mouth. A couple of police officers were talking to the few people who hadn't been ill. The officers' faces were scrunched up in disgust as they asked questions. The people they were questioning seemed to be mumbling through their hands—good luck understanding what they were saying. I chuckled, even though it wasn't appropriate. Why didn't they interview them outside? It was almost as ridiculous as a *Monty Python* skit.

Beren, who was leading us, hurried to reach the front doors, and soon, we were out in the cold night air, sprinkling rain dampening the footpath. When we'd gone about a block, Sarah walked normally and took the bandage off her head. I couldn't be patient any longer. "What the hell happened? What aren't you telling Liv and me?"

Will created a bubble of silence. "I've notified Angelica, but it's not an official PIB case yet. We found magic at the scene, but there are a few witches on staff, and a couple of models. There's nothing to say the magic signatures weren't just from people using their magic normally."

Sarah frowned. "My friend isn't a witch. She couldn't have just popped away. And millions of pounds worth of jewellery's gone missing. Evelyn had hired it out for the show."

"Won't she get into trouble from the jewellery owners? She didn't look too worried." At least, that was my take on her demeanour.

"You don't know her, Lily. She's three times more vivacious normally. You have no idea." Well, that was worrying. If she hadn't been holding back, would she have jumped Will in front of everyone?

Will said, "We checked with one of the two security guards who were hired to protect the jewels, and he said it was all insured, but it would mean a steep increase in premiums for the company who hired them out.... That's if they can even get insurance again. This is the second theft in six months they've had to claim on."

"Are they being targeted?" I asked.

We stopped to cross the road, and Will pressed the button. "Could be. In any case, we're better off having this discussion in the boardroom with Ma'am."

"Don't forget stupid Agent Chad Williamson the Third." Beren rolled his eyes.

Will made an unimpressed face. "Yeah, thanks for reminding me."

Chad, a highly incompetent agent from New York, had been put in charge by the big bosses of the PIB, and even though Ma'am had proven herself during the last case, they'd decided to keep him. Two of the artefacts that were stolen last month hadn't been recovered, and that was one of their excuses for punishing Ma'am. The real reason was likely because one of the directors had a personal vendetta against her. Politics sucked. I ignored the shudder that travelled through me—as long as Regula Pythonissam didn't have those artefacts, we'd be good. What were the chances they'd connected with the criminal who'd stolen them before we'd caught him? Hmm, sometimes it was better not to ask.

Back at the car, we all hopped in. The drive home was rather quiet, except for my stomach, which had recovered from the earlier grossness. "I'm hungry."

Will chuckled. "Of course you are. And, look, there's a McDonald's. How convenient."

I smiled. "The universe is listening to my stomach. Can we do drive-through?"

"Yes, but if you get anything on my upholstery, there'll be consequences."

"Hmm, that doesn't sound all that bad. Maybe I'll spill

something on porpoise." I let out a dolphin cackle—I had no idea if porpoises made much noise—and laughed, imagining someone spilling food on a porpoise.

Everyone groaned. I could see Sarah in the rear-view mirror, smiling. "One thing I can count on to cheer me up is your questionable sense of humour."

I turned to look at her. "Glad to meet expectations. You're welcome."

We arrived home at nine thirty and found Angelica in one of the armchairs in front of the fire in the sitting room. She rose and came to greet Sarah while the rest of us settled on the Chesterfields. "So good to see you, dear." Angelica made her way over to us and sat next to Will, and Sarah sat next to Liv on the other chair. "Well, what are you waiting for? Fill me in."

Will regarded her with a serious expression. "You don't want to go to headquarters?" He hadn't spelled it out, but she would've known he meant we were under orders to run everything by Chad.

"I want to hear everything first. I don't like being the last to know. Knowledge is power, and I'd like to have time to process everything before we decide how to handle it. That way, we can steer Chad where we need him to go. I'm afraid he's not happy with our original agreement and has been asking to attend crime scenes more often than not. His suggestions on how we should handle things are pushing my patience to the limit." As if solving crimes wasn't hard enough, and now he was adding to Ma'am's stress. Ma'am pursed her lips. Her chest rose with an aggravated breath. She mumbled something, and her magic tingled my scalp. A cup of tea appeared in her hands, and she took a sip before relaxing her shoulders back. She looked at Will. "Begin at the point you arrive. Leave nothing out—sometimes the devil is in the details. And, Sarah, I expect you to give me your experience too."

They both gave a nod. Will went first. He described us taking our seats, the fashion show, the lights going out, and his and Beren's response. "It was chaos backstage. Four people had been hit on the head—Sarah being one of them. Everyone else was just confused and some panicking. I went straight to Sarah, who was being helped by a make-up artist and another model. Beren checked on the other three victims, two of whom had been totally knocked out and were still unconscious. Once I ascertained Sarah was okay and that she'd been hit after the lights went out, I did a quick other-sight scan of the area and picked up multiple magical signatures.

"One of the unconscious people was a security guard. His mate hadn't been touched. He was able to confirm what jewellery had been taken and that it was insured. When I left, he was on the phone to the owners of the stolen loot. More concerning is that one model is missing. We can assume that she's in on the theft."

"No." Sarah sat up straight, and she shook her head. "Luisa is not a thief. She's a successful model who earns six figures a year. She's one of my best friends on the circuit." She folded her arms. "There's just no way. If anything, she's been kidnapped."

Will gave her a sympathetic look. He probably thought he was the wiser one, and, yeah, he had plenty of experience with criminals, but he was being condescending with his preconceived opinion. How disappointing. "You can never really know a person, sis. Remember when Uncle Patrick tried to fleece Dad with that share scheme?"

She huffed. "It's not the same. This is a well-known model we're talking about. She's famous in Italy, her home country. She's been in famous fashion campaigns. People would recognise her. It would be hard for her to hide. Besides, she's not a witch. Whoever did this would've had to have popped in and out."

"Why? Because we couldn't find any trace of her? The lights were out for a good two or three minutes. That's plenty of time to escape with the loot."

"Nope. I'm not buying it. How would she knock out all those people? Besides, she'd never hit me."

He raised his brows. "How do you know? Maybe she did it to throw off the scent because everyone would listen to you defend her. At this stage, she's missing and so is the jewellery. I can only get two if I add one and one together." The urge was strong to correct him, but I wasn't going to tell him that zero and two also added up to two because today was stressful enough without getting yelled at. "Before we keep arguing about this, let's check the security cameras, see if they picked anything up. If she left, we'll get her on the street."

"I stand by my assessment of her. Why don't you guys do some more digging before you decide?" Her face softened. "Please, Will. I'm not naïve; I get that sometimes people do things for desperate reasons and that some people are good at fooling everyone around them, but this isn't that scenario. Can you just consider my character reference of her? If you discount the possibility of anyone else having done this, you're potentially letting someone off scot-free."

Will gave Angelica a quick look before saying, "Okay, but we can't ignore facts; that's all I'm saying. You wouldn't be the first person to be blindsided by a friend."

"Maybe not, but wait. You'll see." Stalemate. I hoped for

Sarah's sake that Will was wrong. As much as I trusted her assessment, I could also see how obvious it was that her friend had done it, likely with an accomplice, but she was probably in on it. I was keeping my opinion to myself for a change—we hardly got to see Sarah, and I didn't want to waste the time she was with us arguing.

Angelica looked at Sarah. "Please give me your version of events, and no assumptions, please, just facts."

Sarah pursed her lips. "Of course. I'd just changed into my next outfit and was waiting to get my earrings handed to me when the lights went out. Luisa had been standing right next to me, in the process of getting her diamond necklace for the next outfit. I heard her scream, and then someone whacked my head. I fell. I think I blacked out for a moment. By the time I opened my eyes, the lights were back on, and a few others were screaming or crying. Lavender, one of the make-up artists, saw me and immediately tried to help. He wasn't injured. Pretty much immediately after, Will and Beren arrived."

"Thank you, Sarah. Do you have a photo of her?" Angelica magicked her teacup and saucer away.

"Yes." Sarah went through her phone and pulled up a pic. After Angelica looked at it, she handed it around to all of us. Once Sarah had her phone back, Angelica turned to me. "Lily, was there a burst of magic you'd recognise when the lights went out, or afterwards?"

"That's a tricky one. There was quite a bit of magic flying around throughout the show. Several witches were there, and I doubt I could pick anyone's magic out of the bunch because I wasn't really paying attention." My mouth fell open. "That's right! Maybe a minute or two after the lights went out, there was a really powerful jolt of magic. I remember it because it was like getting smacked in the back of the head. Other than the force of it, I'm not sure there was much else specific I can remember. Maybe just that it was… I don't know… efficient? I don't even know if that makes sense, but it was like the witch is someone who likes doing things well, but they're not a time-waster." Angelica looked at me as if I wasn't making much sense, but what else was new? At least I wasn't in trouble.

"Okay, then. We'll need to see security video of the night."

Beren sat forward. "There was a witch policeman. I got his name, just in case. I'll get in touch with him. The security footage is probably with the police by now. He can get us a copy."

"Good work." Angelica's mouth settled into a straight line. Not quite a smile, but happy enough. The rest of her face might as well have been Botoxed for all it gave away. "Right, well, I think that's all we're going to get for now. Let's go to headquarters. Since you were all there, you can all come. I can't wait to get Chad back out to work late—he's allergic to overtime. He's going to be so happy." So, that's what it took to get her smiling. She stood. "Don't worry, team, we'll make it quick." She made her doorway and left. We followed.

CHAPTER 2

The next morning, Angelica knocked on my bedroom door at eight. Gah, too early. Will groaned—it was his first sleep-in for at least two weeks, well, an "almost" sleep-in. I sat up and called out, "What is it?"

"Are you decent?"

I pulled the covers up to my neck. "Yes."

She opened the door and poked her head in. She was already wearing her uniform, and her hair was tightly secured in her bun. Talk about a morning person, although she was always immaculate, even at midnight. Okay, so she was an all-the-time person. "We have the security video. I've alerted Chad. We're meeting at headquarters at eight thirty. Up you get."

I yawned. "Okay."

"Where's your enthusiasm for the new day, dear?"

"It doesn't exist, just like my sleep-in."

She chuckled. "See you two downstairs in ten."

After she shut the door, Will and I got up, brushed our

teeth, and dressed. At least popping clothes on with magic was quick. We were waiting in the downstairs hallway ten minutes later, coffees in hand. Angelica came out of the living room. "Ready?" We both answered in the affirmative, made our doorways, and stepped through into the PIB reception room.

Gus answered the door and grinned. "Morning, all. Busy day ahead?"

"Always," Ma'am replied. "Always."

"Morning, Gus!" Gus was a familiar sight and one that gave me comfort. As long as Gus was here, things were normal, well, as normal as they could be in an organisation full of witches.

"Morning, Miss Lily. Have a lovely day and stay safe." He shut the door behind us, but because Ma'am and Will were with me, he didn't need to show me anywhere.

"Will do. You too." I gave him a wave as we walked off. Was it mean that I was happy to have avoided another gross conversation?

We were the first to arrive at the conference room. Will sat to the right of Ma'am's spot at the head of the table, and I sat next to him. We left the other side for my brother. When Ma'am sat in James's seat, it brought me back to reality. I frowned. "Yes, dear, exactly. That's not my seat anymore." She pressed her lips together and folded her arms. It was slack of me to forget since we'd only been in here last night. *Idiot, Lily.*

Within five minutes, everyone else arrived. Chad wiggled his fingers, and Ma'am's old chair at the head of the table slid out enough that he could sit. Did he think he'd impressed us? The weakest of witches could do that. It was easy to do it the non-witch way, so most witches didn't bother. It wasn't like he had his hands full.

Imani and Liv both bent to give me a hug before taking

their seats on my side of the table, and James, Beren, and Millicent sat on the other. Once everyone was quiet, Ma'am opened her mouth but shut it again so forcefully, I heard her teeth clack together. She wouldn't be leading this meeting—that honour would go to Chad.

Chad smiled. "Welcome, all. Great to see you again so soon. Except…" He swivelled his head and stared at me. "Why are *you* here? You're not an agent?"

Wow, good pick up, Chad. Before I could answer, Will jumped in, obviously fearful of what I'd say. I smirked. "She contracts to us, and since Lily was there at the time, we're including her in discussions. She has clearance. Let's not forget that she helped us catch Shamus last month. If it wasn't for Lily, who knows what could've happened. There'd probably be a whole lot more witch criminals on the loose." Aw, it was nice to be appreciated. Chad wrinkled his brow, obviously not convinced. If that hadn't convinced him, nothing likely would.

Ma'am cleared her throat. "Excuse me, Agent Williamson the Third. I'm sure you've got more important things to do today, seeing as how you're so important. I'd hate to waste your time with silly things. Shouldn't we just get on with the meeting? I know Agent Bianchi has to get back to something else he was working on, as does Agent Jawara."

Ma'am's ploy to distract him worked. How unsurprising. He wasn't hard to manipulate, thank goodness. The only thing Ma'am hadn't managed was to get him to butt out of her cases. He nodded slowly. "Yes, of course. I get so caught up in the exciting things that I forget all the other duties on my plate are just as significant, and I do have a lot of them. When you called me this morning, you mentioned some security footage."

"Indeed, I did." A small pulse of Ma'am's magic vibrated

along my scalp, and a TV screen appeared on the wall behind Chad. She pointed at it. "There we go."

He turned his chair around with magic, but instead of making it lift off the floor, hover, and turn, he stood, made it turn around, then sat. Imani was trying not to smile. Our gazes met, and we shared a "look." James sent me a death glare across the table. I pressed my lips together and tried not to smile. Okay, so we were being juvenile, but how else was I going to survive Chad's stupidity whilst he lorded it over everyone? Ma'am deserved to be calling the shots, and through no fault of her own was beholden to this idiot.

The video played with no sound. The screen was divided into four images—each a different camera in the building. Two showed internal areas and two external, the external cameras showing the only two entries into the building. After watching for over twenty minutes, it was clear that no one had left during that time, or soon afterwards. Angelica magicked the screen to pause. "As you can see, it's likely someone made a doorway and left. Police were stationed around the building all night and took stock of everyone who came or went. Sarah's friend is still missing, and her credit cards and phone haven't been used. Will magicked a sample of blood from the scene, and we've managed to match it to the missing woman's health records." I had to wonder how they'd found her records, but I supposed they were the PIB—they had access to so much that the rest of us didn't.

"How come Sarah's not here?" When Chad whiplashed his head around to stare at me, I realised I shouldn't have called attention to myself.

Ma'am got in before he could hassle me again. "She hasn't got clearance for this meeting. Last night was different because we needed to get her statement."

"Oh, okay." We'd left Sarah asleep. Now I felt like a crappy friend. I should have checked in on her to make sure she was okay. Beren had healed her, but you never knew—maybe he was as fallible as normal doctors. She could have even been upset about her friend.

Chad had turned his chair back. He put his elbows on the table and steepled his fingers. He'd make a good comedic supervillain à la Dr Evil in *Austin Powers*. Instead of ordering Ma'am to destroy the world, he asked, "What do you propose we do now?"

Ma'am magicked a glass of water to herself and took a sip before answering. "We're going to question the owner of the jewellery, the designer who was running the fashion show, everyone who was part of it, and Luisa's friends. We need to establish whether anyone had a motive to harm Luisa or Evelyn the designer or a motive to make off with millions of pounds' worth of diamonds and gold. We'd scout London second-hand dealers, but I'm afraid we wouldn't have much luck."

Chad folded his arms and leaned back. "Why do you say that? I would've thought it was a good place to start."

"If our perpetrator is a witch, they could have travelled anywhere in the world to sell their heist. Obviously, it would take a witch of great stamina to travel across the ocean to the US or Australia, but, still, putting a call out to every second-hand dealer in Europe and the UK would be a huge ask."

"But not impossible." I wanted to wipe the self-satisfied smile off his face with a rotting fish. Was that too aggressive? Hmm, maybe I needed more coffee.

Ma'am gave him a fake smile, the one she reserved for children and idiots. "Not impossible, just time-consuming and a poor use of our resources. I will put a notice out to shops in the UK, of course, and I'll liaise with our other European offices, but they're much smaller than headquarters, and they don't have the resources either. I'm afraid as good as we are, we're still under-resourced, and we must take that into consideration when planning our investigations."

It was his turn to give her his fake smile. I didn't know him, but that half-grimace thing he was doing with his mouth meant he either had a nasty stomach ache, or he didn't like what he'd just heard. "I can assure you that I know what to take into consideration. I've learnt an unbelievable amount over the last few weeks. In fact, I insist, and to make sure it runs smoothly, I'm going to put you in charge of contacting all the second-hand gold and gems dealers in Europe." Ma'am put her poker face on lockdown. She didn't as much as twitch a facial muscle. The rest of us held our collective breaths, waiting for her reaction.

It didn't come, but I had no doubt it would… one day. Hopefully I'd be there to see him get his comeuppance. He was being reckless, and now the investigation was going to take way longer for nothing except for him to gain the upper hand on Ma'am. Ego was the cause of so many bad actions. But what if he was stymying her on purpose? Maybe the director who wanted her gone wasn't finished with her yet. My shoulders slumped. As if Ma'am didn't have enough to deal with.

Ma'am still hadn't answered. Chad looked at James, no doubt rallying for support. James showed his solidarity with Ma'am by engaging his own poker face. Chad raised his chin in the air, as if in defiance. "Right, then. You have my orders." His voice wasn't as confident as before. Had he realised he was about to tiptoe through croc-infested waters? He stood, maybe feeling braver because he was looking down on Ma'am, and he was in a better position to run at a moment's notice. "Carry them out. Update me in two days. Now, if you'll excuse me, I have an important meeting to attend." He made a doorway and skedaddled. I would've too, if I were him.

Once he'd left, Ma'am created a bubble of silence and growled. "That incompetent fool. The director Mr Brosnan's put him up to this, I bet. Anything to make me fail. Well, I won't have it. Not on my watch. Solving this crime is our number-one priority. Even if I'm tied up with a ridiculous goose chase, I want all of you to continue in the manner we're supposed to. Agent Bianchi, I'd like you to organise the interviews. Lily, I'd like Agent Jawara to accompany you to the scene of the crime to take some photos. You can use these police passes we have for special occasions." A plastic ID card stating that I was with the police investigation unit appeared on the table in front of me. Another card sat in front of Imani.

Imani was already in uniform, but I'd dressed in normal clothes, thinking I'd only be going to the meeting. I drew my magic and changed clothes. Thankfully, nothing went wrong—I wasn't suddenly sitting there with nothing on. It had taken a few days to get my confidence back after the curse was cured. Imani stood. Ma'am said, "Here are the coordinates for the closest landing spot and the address of the building. They're about five blocks from each other. Good luck, ladies. When you're done, report to Liv. She'll coordinate the information and let either James or me know."

All the details appeared in my mind as big golden numbers and letters. Imani gave me a nod. "Let's go." I smiled and magicked my camera to myself. Then I plonked the numbers on my doorway and stepped through.

We came out in a small public toilet. Dumb me didn't wait long enough for Imani to go through, and when I landed in the cubicle, I bumped into her. She fell forward and hit the door, palms first. She turned her head and gave me an "are you stupid?" look.

I bit my bottom lip. "Sorry." She shook her head and shooed me back so she could open the door. I exited straight after her to the enquiring gaze of a teenager. Great, she probably thought we'd been in there doing stuff we shouldn't be. My cheeks heated. Travelling wasn't all it was cracked up to be.

As we exited, the girl called out, "Wash your hands, filthy heathens!" Oh God. The indignity travelled down my neck, and I wanted to take my jacket off and cool the mortification. Imani laughed. "Your fault, girl. Next time, wait a minute."

"Sorry. I forgot. Oh, look, a squirrel!" Full distraction-mode activated. A cute grey squirrel ran up the wide trunk of a tree in a small park. That was one thing I loved about London—so many areas of green, which was unexpected in such a big city. There were pockets big and small filled with grass, trees, and sometimes a park bench and meandering path.

The grey sky threatened rain, but, thankfully, it was still dry. It took a few minutes to reach the place of the fashion parade. The large glass doors at the front didn't open. I frowned. "Looks like they're closed today. Are they for event bookings only?"

Imani shrugged. "Oh, hang on. Is that someone inside?" We put our faces to the glass and peered in. The floor appeared to have been cleaned, thank goodness. I shuddered in remembrance. A woman walked through the room, oblivious of us. Imani rapped on the glass with her knuckles. The woman, dressed in a blue pencil skirt and white shirt, halted and peered at us. Imani made a "come here" wave.

The woman put her hands on her hips, as if she were

annoyed, then decided to see what we wanted. She opened the door. "Yes, what can I help you with?"

Imani flashed her ID card. "We're from the Special Investigations Unit. We're here to photograph the scene from last night's crime."

"No one told me you were coming." She folded her arms. "I don't have to let you in."

"I'm afraid you do." Imani pulled a piece of paper from her trouser pocket. "This is official documentation giving us access. If you hinder our access, you can be arrested for obstruction of an investigation." Imani raised a brow and handed the woman the paper.

After reading it, she pursed her lips, annoyance radiating from her glare. "Fine." She let us in but didn't offer to show us where it was. At least I already knew.

"This way," I said to Imani before heading to the stairs.

We hurried up. Luckily, all the doors we had to go through were unlocked. Police tape cordoned off the door from the audience area to backstage, but no police were here. We ducked under the tape and entered.

"It was dark when it all went down. I have no idea if I'll be able to take any photos that help."

Imani made a bubble of silence. "But you can get photos of what happened beforehand?"

"Yep. Hmm, also, I can ask if Sarah's friend committed the crime, kind of. I'll ask my magic to show me who stole the jewellery. If she doesn't show up, she's innocent."

Imani smiled. "You're more useful than you know."

"Ha, thanks."

The room hadn't been tidied from the debacle that was last night. They probably had to keep it "as is" until the police were totally finished with it. I lifted my camera and took the lens cap off. Drawing on the magic river, I said, "Show me who took the jewellery."

The room was suddenly full of models in various stages of undress. A hairdresser was adjusting someone's hair. Sarah's friend was standing near the security guard who had been hit. She was staring at him. Nothing seemed to be in her hands, though. There were so many people crowded around that I had no idea who the hell the culprit was. This was ridiculous. My magic couldn't single someone out of a group shot, unfortunately. As far as my magic was concerned, it was showing me who stole it. At least we'd narrowed things down to about twenty people—and that was sarcasm, just in case you couldn't tell. I snapped a few shots, walked around, and took more from every angle.

I lowered my camera. "I'm done."

"And?"

"Not much help. The perpetrator is in there, at least, or my camera would have shown nothing, but it's also included everyone else in the room with them." I handed her the camera.

She flicked through the photos. She looked up at me with a "what can you do?" look and handed the camera back. I sighed. I might as well not have taken any photos. Hmm. "Actually, come out here. I think I can do something else that might work." It wasn't as if I had to photograph the person in the act of committing the crime. There was unlikely a moment the perpetrator was by themselves in this room, but if it was a model or the host, they would have been on stage by themselves at some point.

I hurried into the other room, stood in front of the first row of chairs, and faced the stage. "Show me who stole the jewels." I really hoped it wasn't Sarah's friend.

Bummer.

Luisa stood at the end of the catwalk, posing, the only one on the stage. It was the second before a new model would have come through the curtains. I heavy sighed and snapped off the shots. I handed Imani the camera. "We have our thief."

Imani perused the photos. "By your reaction, I'm assuming it's Sarah's friend?"

"Yep." Sarah was not going to be happy. "Can we tell her before we tell Ma'am?"

Imani gave back the camera. "No. That goes against the rules, Lily. We can't risk her warning Luisa."

"It's not as if Luisa wouldn't know she's wanted by the police—she's just pulled off a major heist, for goodness' sake."

She shook her head and looked at me. She opened her mouth, then closed it. I cocked my head to the side. "What, what were you going to say?"

"Nothing."

"Don't nothing me. I want to know. You can't almost tell me something and expect I'll sleep tonight not knowing." I gave her a look of mock horror.

She rolled her eyes. "Fine, but do not repeat this to Sarah, or I'll kill you." She narrowed her eyes, likely hammering home her point. "We might be able to use Sarah to help find her. If we announce she's wanted, maybe she'll try and warn her. If she makes contact, we can trace the call."

"I can't believe you'd do that! You know Sarah would help if we asked."

She raised a brow. "Oh, but do you? Will her loyalty to her friend win out, especially if she doesn't believe she did it?"

I chewed my bottom lip. She had a point. Plus, it wouldn't be my job on the line if Imani went against protocol. "Fine. You're right." Gah, it hurt to say that.

She smiled. "You better believe it. Let's check in with Liv."

I followed Imani down the stairs. We bade the cranky woman goodbye, then went to the nearest public toilets and made our doorways to headquarters. Liv was in her and Millicent's office, and, as a nice surprise, Millicent was there too. She looked up from her laptop as we entered. "Hello, ladies. That was quick."

Imani and I sat in front of her desk. I let Imani do the talking since she was the actual agent. "We needed to check in with Liv." She turned to her. "Lily got us some great photos." I handed my camera to Liv.

She took it. "Ooh, let's see." As soon as she saw the photo of Luisa, she deflated, her shoulders slumping, and her body sliding lower in her chair. "Oh, wow. Sarah is not going to be happy."

"I know, right?"

Millicent looked at us with a quizzical expression. "Did you confirm it was her friend?" All of us nodded, which might have made for a comical scene were we not talking about something so serious.

"Thanks, ladies," said Liv. "I'll get this info to James. Can you magic the picture onto my computer?"

I smiled. "Sure." Since anyone could have taken that photo during the parade, no one would wonder how we came to have it, and only those who knew about my secret talent would have any idea what it signified—Luisa's guilt. "So, who's going to tell Sarah?" Everyone stared at me. "What? Why me? You've known her for longer, Mill. She's your husband's best friend's sister."

She smiled and shook her head. "I'm afraid since you're practically her sister-in-law, the honour goes to you. Will, as sweet as he can be, won't be tactful enough." She had a point, but I still didn't like having to do it.

I sighed. "Fine. When do you want me to do the deed?"

"I'd leave it till we get the okay from Ma'am, love," Imani said.

"Okay. Now what?" I was hoping they'd have something else for me to do because I didn't fancy going home and pretending in front of Sarah that I didn't know what was going on. What a crappy thing to happen when we were supposed to be spending time together. She wouldn't have long here. This whole thing really sucked.

Liv shrugged. "Um… until Ma'am gets back to us with more work, there's really nothing for you to do. Sorry."

I looked at Millicent. "Do you have anything for me to do? Filing, polishing shoes, washing cars?"

She chuckled, then regret settled on her face. "I'm sorry, Lily, but I don't have anything either." She looked at her watch. "Maybe Imani can spare half an hour to accompany you and Sarah to Costa for a coffee and double-chocolate muffin?" She knew me well.

"Bribing me with a visit to Costa will get you off the hook… for now."

"Okay, lovie, let's go." Imani stood. "I'll check in when I get back."

Millicent smiled. "Have fun."

Liv waved. "Say hi to Sarah for me."

"Will do." Unfortunately, I wasn't allowed to say much else. Lying to my friends was not on my list of favourite things to do. Another reason being an agent didn't suit me. Yes, it was for a good reason, but my heart was too soft. Damn heart.

CHAPTER 3

It was early to bed after a lovely night with Will and Sarah where we all managed to avoid talking about the "incident." Going to dinner and a movie helped distract me, although Sarah had been quieter than usual, probably worried about her friend. The next morning, Angelica made a bubble of silence over breakfast. My stomach dropped. Here it came.

Angelica carefully placed her teacup on her saucer and fixed a gentle gaze on Sarah. Sarah stiffened. "What? You haven't found her body, have you?" Anyone who knew Angelica knew she didn't do nice unless there were important reasons.

"No, nothing like that, dear, but you might want to brace yourself." Angelica regarded her for a moment, and satisfied she was sufficiently braced, continued. "Lily took some photos yesterday that prove Luisa was involved. I'm sorry."

Sarah's eyes widened. She turned to me, her gaze desperately seeking what I couldn't give her. My sad frown said it all.

She blinked and shook her head. "I still can't believe it." She sat back and folded her arms. "Show me the photos."

I looked to Angelica, who nodded. I magicked my camera to myself, turned it on, and handed it to her. She slowly unfolded her arms and leaned forward to grab it from across the table. Sarah flicked through the photos, then looked up at me. "This doesn't prove anything. You have a photo of her on the catwalk. How does that mean she's guilty?"

Sarah was one of the few people who knew how my talent worked, but maybe I had never explained it properly. "Before I take the photo, I ask my magic a question. In this case, I asked who stole the jewels. It showed me Luisa. It doesn't have to be the person in the middle of performing the act, which, in this case, happened in the dark. I had to think of another way to find out, so I went into the other room and asked. This is what I got. My magic has never been wrong before." I stood and gently prised the camera out of her hands. "I'm sorry, Sarah. I really am. I didn't want it to be her either." I magicked my camera back to my room.

Her shoulders sagged. "I just can't believe it."

Will put his arm around his sister and pulled her into his side. "Sometimes we just don't know people like we think we do. I'm sorry." She sagged against him, defeated. Will and I shared a sad look. I couldn't imagine how I'd feel if I found out Liv or Imani were criminals. It would be devastating wondering if I'd never known who they really were. You'd question everything, your whole friendship.

Angelica's cup clinked on the saucer as she placed it down after having another sip of tea. "Maybe she wouldn't have done this a year ago. It doesn't mean everything you knew about her was a lie, but maybe something has changed recently. Can you think of anything happening in her life right now that might have made her do this?"

Sarah's brow furrowed, and she chewed her bottom lip, thinking. After a minute, she slid out of Will's embrace and sat straighter. She shook her head. "I don't know. About six months ago, she broke up with her wealthy boyfriend. He used to pay for a lot of stuff for her—not that she ever asked him to, and, in fact, sometimes it made her uncomfortable. She didn't want to be a kept woman. He'd become controlling with other things and wanted her to give up modelling. Modelling is her passion in life, so she broke up with him. But I know she's earning enough money to pay her bills—at least, I thought she was."

"How did she take the break-up?" Will asked.

"She wasn't happy about it, because even though Lorenzo was being difficult, she still loved him."

Will took a sip of coffee, trying to act casual. "Was she upset enough to abuse any substances?" Unfortunately for him, it didn't have the desired effect of swaying her to his way of thinking if the disgusted look on her face was anything to go by. "Drug addictions eat through the cash."

Sarah raised her voice. "What?! No! How can you even suggest that? She's a down-to-earth girl from a middle-class neighbourhood in Florence. I've never seen her touch drugs, even though there's always plenty to go around at parties and events. She drinks a glass or two of wine, or gin and tonic, but that's it."

Will gave up trying to look like he wasn't going to ask the hard questions. He turned in his seat to face her, his brow furrowed. "People can hide drug habits. You might not even realise unless you're living with the person. Have her moods changed recently? Has she been cagey about anything? Even if you don't want to tell us anything now, just think about it. Please?"

"I don't spend all my time with her, but when we're doing the same shows, we share a hotel room. I've spent seven out of the last fourteen weeks with her, on and off. I would know." She folded her arms again and scowled. So, she wasn't going to budge, and maybe she was right. This was getting us nowhere.

"Um, I know you want to solve this crime as soon as possible, but why don't we give Sarah a break? Maybe she's right? In the meantime, we aren't going to get much time with her, and I've been slacking on the exercise lately, so how about the three of us go for a run?" I couldn't do things by myself outside the house because of Regula Pythonissam, and Will had been too busy to go for a regular run with me, unless I wanted to get up at six, which was a big, fat no. I wanted to see where I was running, or I was likely to trip and kill myself, plus it had been insanely cold at that time of the morning. Summer couldn't come soon enough.

Sarah managed a small smile. "I'd like that, actually. I could do with dispelling some of this *negative*"—she narrowed her eyes at Angelica, then at Will—"energy."

Will raised a brow but wisely said nothing. "Okay. Let's do that."

"I'll see you when you get back," Angelica said. I couldn't help but hear the warning in her voice. Sarah's battle wasn't over. Not by a long shot.

We returned from our run, finding that Angelica had already gone to work. Will showered and left. After Sarah and I showered and dressed, we sat in the living room in front of the fire with our coffees. She looked at me. "Thanks for that before." She shook her head. "When Will and Angelica get hold of a bone, they won't let go."

I smiled. "I know, but it's their job. I get where they're coming from, and maybe they're right, but maybe you are too. My magic says it was her, but maybe she had a good reason? I'm not going to judge."

"Thanks." She sighed. "Look, as much as I can't stand everyone insisting it's her, I get it—it looks like she stole that jewellery. I just can't get my head around it. It's not like her at all."

I took a deep breath, hoping not to push her too far. "Can we just assume for a minute that she did take the jewellery? You can just pretend, okay?"

She gave a wry smile. "Yes, Miss Diplomat. I can do that."

"What if she was working with someone else? Who is she close to that was there that night?" Gah, was it only two nights ago? It seemed like a week ago. So much had happened since then, or, rather, I'd done so much since then.

Sarah stared into the fire for a couple of minutes before turning to me. "There's another model she's good friends with, although I don't really get on with her—Saskia. And she's close to Evelyn."

Fake eyelashes and hot-pink eyeshadow came to mind. "That's the designer, right?"

"Yep."

"Is Saskia a witch?"

"Yes, but Evelyn isn't. And we don't know whether there was magic involved."

"True, but it would be a damn sight easier for a witch to help pull this off. Your friend wasn't seen leaving by anyone or any cameras. Unless she hid and left later, or disguised herself and left with everyone else? Is there anywhere to hide in that place?"

"I have no idea. It's a big building, so probably. But surely the police would have done a thorough search." She frowned. "I hate to say it, but you're making some good points. I still don't believe it, but Ma'am and Will will eat this stuff up."

I reached across and put my hand on her shoulder. "I'm not trying to be awful, honestly. It's just a natural talent I have." I gave her a helpless smile.

She blew out a loud breath and gave me a lopsided smile. "I know." She sipped her coffee, then sat up straighter and pinned me with her gaze. "I played pretend. Now it's your turn."

Oh, she was good. "I suppose I'm pretending that she didn't do it." And it was only pretending because my magic was never wrong, but if you couldn't humour your friends when they needed it, what kind of friend were you?

"Yes. So, let's just say it wasn't her. Who else had motive and opportunity?"

I shrugged. "Potentially everyone who was there, including you." I laughed. "Are you planning to shower me with diamonds on my birthday?"

She chuckled and waggled her eyebrows. "Isn't that my brother's job?"

I rolled my eyes. "Yeah, yeah." I cleared my throat, hoping to change the subject. Diamonds were nice and sparkly, but there were more important things to spend money on. And I didn't want her to think I was desperate to marry Will, because I definitely wasn't. We hadn't even lived together by ourselves yet—our whole living with each other thing had been in Angelica's house… with Angelica present. Not that I would learn much about him if we shacked up just the two of us, but young and with no kids on the horizon, there was no pressure. Also, who knew what would happen in the next year or two? The way we were going with the PIB and our search for what happened to my parents, one of us could be dead by then. I sighed. I needed to stop being so morose.

"Lily, are you okay?" Sarah's brows drew down.

"Oh, yes. Sorry. Just drifting off with the fairies."

"As long as you're back now."

I saluted. "Reporting for duty."

She smiled. "Great. Now, I just know you would love to ask me who, in particular, had motive."

"Of course. Who had the motive, other than your friend?"

"Thanks for asking. Well, Evelyn, of course."

I stared at her, perplexed. "What do you mean, of course? It's not like she was wearing a slogan on her top saying, 'I want to steal jewellery.'"

"Well, if someone had just asked, I could have told them, but you all seem to have made up your minds."

"I don't know that that's fair. My magic's never wrong, and Will and Ma'am are just doing their jobs. They still have to question everyone, and I would think that if anyone seems suss, they'll investigate further. And, seriously, she's the only one missing and so is the jewellery."

She rolled her eyes. "You're not doing a very good job of pretending. I haven't finished yet."

"Sorry. Please continue." She was right—I was doing a crappy job. I just needed to keep my mouth shut for a few more minutes. Surely I could manage that?

"As I was saying… Evelyn was broke. She's been losing money over the last few years, and she had to borrow it to set everything up for this show. It was her second-last hurrah, so to speak. If she doesn't get some good trade from this show and the next one, she'll be all out of money. And before you ask how I know all this, she paid the models before the show because someone heard her drunkenly mention it at a dinner a couple of months ago. Word gets around in our industry."

I let that sink in. Right, so she had motive, but she wasn't a witch, which meant the normal police would still be left to handle it. If there really had been no magic used to steal the items or there wasn't a witch, it was out of our jurisdiction. "Okay. What about Saskia? What's her story, and why do you think she might be involved?"

"She's not overly successful yet—she's eighteen and has only been at this for six months. I know she loves to buy pretty things. Apart from the fact that she always has some new two-thousand-pound designer bag or thousand-pound pair of shoes, Luisa's told me she's in debt up to her eyeballs. She's addicted to the high-end lifestyle."

"If she's a witch, couldn't she just buy the materials and magic herself copycat stuff?" That's what I would do. In fact, why didn't I? I knew: it's because I was such a dag. Comfort usually came before looks with me, and I was too lazy to bother swapping out handbags all the time. I had *stuff* in my handbag, and having to transfer it every time I wanted a change would be irritating. Not to mention the rubbish of old receipts, tissues, train tickets from before we had tap-on and tap-off cards, and shopping lists, and that one time there was that small melted Easter Egg I found in August… I'd be forever cleaning it out. No thank you.

Sarah shook her head, her silky, long ponytail bouncing from side to side. "You've got to be joking. Designer stuff is like a religion for a lot of these women. To be honest, I love it too. Some of these designers are producing works of art. I don't often spend a lot, but every now and then, I buy *pieces*—like a stunning handbag or new-season dress. Plus, if I want the work, it's better to look the part, at least when I'm at events or go-sees. I never spend more than I can afford." Sarah was successful, and she'd been working as a model for a few years, time enough to have saved to buy her own two-bedroom flat in London, among other things.

"Is there anyone else you can think of who might be guilty?"

"Nope. That's it. The other obvious answer could be the actual company that supplied the diamond jewellery or their security guards. It wouldn't be the first fraudulent insurance claim that ever was."

"True. I'll trust the PIB to dig through that information and see if any of the company owners is a witch. This is all moot if a human committed the crime. Angelica will stop the investigation." The next part of the conversation was something I hadn't seen coming, and I realised what a worry it could be. I swallowed. "Okay, so still assuming your friend is innocent… what the hell happened to her, and where is she?"

Sarah looked at me, worry bleak in her gaze. "And that's exactly it, Lily. She's missing, and I have the worst feeling."

A pit opened in my stomach. What if Sarah wasn't misguided? What if Luisa was in trouble? I looked at Sarah, wanting to say something comforting, but I had nothing. All I could think of was that she could be right.

Crap.

CHAPTER 4

When Will came home that evening, Sarah and I were having a quiet game of rummy in the kitchen, the mood sombre. He kissed the top of Sarah's head, then sat next to me and gave me a kiss on the lips. "How are my two favourite women?" Full marks to him for being enthusiastic and trying to lighten things.

I gave a half smile. "We're okay. Sarah's worried about her friend, and there's nothing I can do about it, so that's about where we're at."

"I'm sorry. There's nothing more I can do about it, except question suspects, which I've been doing all day. It's not good news, I'm afraid."

Sarah sat up straight and laid her cards face down on the table. Her intense gaze was laser focussed on her brother. "What do you mean? Have you found her?"

"No, no. Nothing like that. It's just… we've run out of witch suspects." He looked at her, waiting for the penny to drop.

She swallowed. "So the PIB is going to drop the case?"

"We're close to that, yes."

That didn't sound good. "Does that mean her fate is in the hands of the normal police?"

Will looked at me. "Don't tell me you think she's innocent?"

"Not necessarily, just that there might be more to this. I'm at least worried about where she is. What if she is guilty, but she was in it with someone else? What if they double-crossed her?"

Sarah frowned. "Lily, I thought you were on my side?"

I sighed. I hated arguing with people. "I am, but I can't ignore my magic. I still think she did it, but I also wonder if she's in trouble—and that's only because of what you said. I trust your judgement."

Sarah pushed her chair back and stood. "I think I'm going to have an early night."

Sadness sat its heavy backside on my chest. She was only here for another day. What if we didn't make peace with her? I was no good at fighting with people I cared about, but I had nothing to say. I couldn't lie to her and pretend I thought her friend didn't do it. Will, thankfully, stood too. He walked around the table and looked down at her. "I'm sorry, Sar." He pulled her into his arms.

She slowly relaxed her stiff body and returned the hug. "I'm just so worried. I feel it in my bones, Will. Something's happened, and I don't mean about things being stolen. I can't give up when I feel like this." She stepped back from him. "If there's nothing you guys can do, I'm going to figure it out myself."

Crap. If I was worried before, I was triply worried now. I didn't know her friend, and I was sorry things had gone wrong, but if anything happened to Sarah…. "You can't! I won't let you." Oh, wow, I hadn't expected that to come out of my mouth. I wasn't usually so demanding.

She raised a brow. "You what?"

My cheeks heated. "I, uh, um…."

"What I think Lily means is that if anything happened to you, we'd both be more than a little upset. And can you imagine what it would do to Mum and Dad?"

She shook her head. "Nothing's going to happen to me, Will. I'm just going to look into it."

He folded his arms, going into big-brother I-know-more-than-you mode. "What are you going to look into? We've interviewed everyone who was there. There are only two witches of interest: they're both still around, and after searching their homes and turning up zilch, both having alibis and no reason to want any harm to come to Luisa, we have nothing, which means you have nothing to look into."

She put her hands on her hips. "Well, Mr Know-It-All, do you know about the two models who are witches who hate her? They weren't walking in the show, but they could have organised this. One of them was in the audience."

Will's brow furrowed, and he pressed his lips together. "Why didn't you tell us this before?"

She raised her chin. "You didn't ask." Her voice became quieter, and she slowly dropped her arms. "And I forgot to mention it. It only just came to me." She gave him a sheepish look.

"Well, hang tight. At least for another day. We haven't been called off the case yet. Maybe there's something I can do to help before you get involved on your own." Will was a good brother. He hardly had time to be sidetracked, but he'd do anything to keep those he loved safe.

She gave him a hug. "Thank you."

Wanting to cap the night off with dessert—which equals happiness—I said, "Who's up for coffee and dessert at Costa?"

Sarah laughed. "I swear if it wasn't for you, Westerham Costa would go broke."

I shrugged. "It's my civic duty to make sure they're around for others to benefit from."

"Are we walking up?" Will asked.

"Why not? I'm sure we could all do with a refreshing stroll." When I said refreshing, I meant freezing, but once I had my snuggly warm coat on, I didn't mind the chill on my face. It was invigorating. But then the excitement rushed away like an outgoing tide, leaving my happiness flopping around struggling for breath on a dry beachfront. Okay, so I was being dramatic, but it was all I had left.

Will's brows drew together. "What's wrong?"

"It's after six. It won't be open." I pouted. The disappointment was crushing.

He laughed. "Drama queen. There's one at Sevenoaks that's open till seven thirty. We can go there."

"You're a genius! I knew there was a reason I kept you around." Crisis averted. Phew!

It took just over fifteen minutes to drive there, order, and hunker down at one of the tables to enjoy our spoils. I got my usual. Will got the same as me, and Sarah bought a cup of tea and a cheese-and-ham croissant. I eyed the savoury snack. "That's not dessert. You're letting the side down."

She chuckled. "I'm more of a savoury person. I mean, I don't mind the occasional sweet thing, but I have to really be in the mood."

"I'll have to eat your life quota of sweet stuff, then." I grinned. I was such a problem solver. Although, my method of solving problems was probably why I wasn't a skinny model and Sarah was. Some things were just more important. I shrugged and bit into my muffin.

As Will and Sarah chatted about their parents and the upcoming cities Sarah was visiting for work, I savoured my coffee and chocolate treat. The warmth and friendly hum of conversation of other patrons was like a gigantic squishy hug. I smiled.

And that's when it started—a subtle magical vibration on my scalp. It lasted mere seconds. I looked around to pinpoint the source of magic, but then *it* hit.

The burn of an electrical zap seared my arm. I cried out and dropped my muffin onto the plate. Diners jerked their heads around to look at me. My tattoo burnt as I gripped my arm to my side and tried to breathe through the pain. I rocked back and forth, head down.

Will grabbed my shoulder. "Lily, are you okay? Speak to me."

"My arm's burning."

He grabbed my hand and pulled it out of my protective hunch. Tears streamed down my face. He pushed my sleeve up. The tattoo outline glowed red, and I was pretty sure I was looking at it without my other sight. Will quickly covered it with both hands. His magic feathered the back of my neck and down my arm. Once it reached my tattoo, the other magic stopped, and the pain dissipated.

I took a shuddering breath and looked up. Sarah was standing, looking around, likely trying to find the culprit. Bloody RP. Will hadn't released my arm or his magic, but the glow had gone. His gaze searched my face. "Are you okay?"

I nodded. "I—I think so." His power stopped, and he removed his grip from the tattoo. My skin looked normal—not burnt, not smoking, not blistered. Sarah had made it to the front door. She opened it and stepped out. I looked at Will. "Don't let her go out there by herself. What if they're still out there?" RP might have orchestrated my pain from somewhere else, but because I'd felt the tingle of magic first, they had to have been nearby. It had been faint, which indicated they were likely outside somewhere close.

"I checked. She has her return to sender up. Actually, we should just leave."

I looked down at the table, at my half-finished coffee and muffin. "No. We're not going anywhere." I channelled my power to create a return-to-sender spell. "I won't cut my lovely night short because of them. They can go jump." Oh, crap. The return to sender was already up. I'd been more efficient than I thought. I swallowed the rush of fear threatening to burst forth.

"Okay. I'll get Sarah and bring her back in. Are you okay if I leave for a moment? You look a little pale."

I gave him my best fake smile. If I told him about this right now, he wouldn't go get Sarah. "I'll be fine. They took me off guard; that's all. I should've known better than to leave the house without my return to sender up." A little white lie went a long way sometimes.

He stood. "I'll be back in a jiffy."

Thankfully, everyone had gone back to minding their own business. I stared out the large front windows, but there wasn't much to see except the faint impression of people outside, as it was way lighter in here than out there. Mostly, the reflection of diners patterned the glass. My stomach was drawn tight, waiting for another attack or for someone to jump up from one of the tables and grab me. But nothing happened. Thankfully,

Will and Sarah came back through the door and returned to the table.

Sarah sat opposite me. "Are you all right? That was awful. You were in so much pain, and I couldn't help." Concern radiated from her gaze.

"I'm okay, but for a moment there, it was excruciating. We really need to get back into our *research*." They would surely know I meant our investigation into RP. We were due to have another meeting tomorrow night. It couldn't come soon enough. Would we ever find out what happened to my parents, or, more to the point, would we find out before they killed me? "Did you see anyone?"

"I swore I saw a man looking in from outside when it happened, but by the time I ran out, he was gone. Sorry."

"Oh my God, don't be! You could've been hurt chasing them anyway. What if they'd attacked you?" The last thing I wanted was for anyone I cared about getting hurt, especially if it was because they were helping me.

She grinned. "Will's taught me a few things over the years. Don't worry—I can look after myself."

Will's phone rang. I sighed. The fun never stopped around here. "Hello, Ma'am." He listened for a moment. "Okay. Bye." He slid the phone back into his pocket. "Let's finish up and go home. We've been summoned. She said you can have five minutes." Gah, how generous. We all had some food left, but there was no way we were going to sit here and enjoy it.

"I give up." I took a last swig of my coffee and picked my muffin up in a napkin. "Let's just go." Sarah gathered her croissant in another napkin, and Will finished the last bit of his double-chocolate muffin. We stood and ventured back out into the cold, clear night. Unfortunately, I couldn't enjoy the mysterious twinkling of far-distant planets as I was trying to observe every which way as we walked, plus I had my paranormal feelers out, waiting for that telltale sign of an impending magical attack. We managed to make it back to the car and home without another incident, but as soon as we got in the door, another joyful announcement awaited—and, yes, that was sarcasm.

Angelica, still in work clothes, met us in the hallway. She made a bubble of silence. "Chad's called off the investigation into the missing jewellery. We have no clues that point to a magical theft, and for once, I agree with his decision." Sparks of anger flickered from her gaze.

"But?" I asked. There was something she wasn't saying but likely wanted to if her non-poker face was anything to go by.

"I've spent the last two days on a wild goose chase of pawn shops all over Europe. I'm bloody exhausted and more than a little annoyed. Chad intended to call the case off at lunchtime today but decided to let me keep going for a while because he 'had other things to do.' Those other things just happened to be a two-hour high tea followed by a visit to Buckingham Palace."

My mouth dropped. "He got to go inside?"

"Pfft, of course not. He saw it from the outside. Then he strolled around the nearby park. He still didn't bother contacting me when he returned to the office. He kindly sent me an email about twenty minutes ago admitting he forgot earlier." Her breaths were deep and forceful, her fists balled. Was she about to have a nervous breakdown?

Will stepped in front of her and held his hand up. A cup of tea appeared in it. He handed it to her. "Here, let's retire to the sitting room. Don't let him get to you. Instead of letting him enrage you, why not channel that anger into something constructive, like how we're going to get rid of him."

She took the tea. "That's very kind of you, William, but if there was an easy way to get rid of him, I'd have done it by now. Your suggestion of tea, however, is an excellent idea." At least her tone was two octaves closer to normal. We followed her to the Chesterfields and sat—Will next to me and Sarah next to her.

I knew this wouldn't help matters, but maybe it would do good if she had something else to focus on. "Since the PIB aren't on that case anymore, do I have permission to help Sarah track down her friend?" Angelica stopped mid-sip and gave me a stern look over her cup.

Sarah jumped in. "I know Lily's magic proved it was Luisa, but something else is going on. I still don't think she took the jewels, at least… well… she isn't the one behind it. She's just not the type. Whoever is behind it could've done something to her. I need to find out. Her family messaged me asking if I know where she is. The police contacted them and have even searched their home in Italy, in case they were hiding her. They're worried. She hasn't been in touch. We won't do anything dangerous. Maybe we could take Will or Imani with us on our hunt?"

Angelica placed her cup on the low table between the couches. She shook her head. "I can't spare them right now, and I don't need anything else to worry about. I'm having enough trouble keeping my job. So, no. I can't support you in this. I'm sorry." She actually did look sorry, and tired. The last few weeks couldn't have been easy for her. She was always so strong that it was easy to forget she struggled just like the rest of us. But Sarah was too emotionally invested.

Sarah stood. "Well, I'll do it with or without anyone's help." She came around the table, bent down, and gave Will a quick hug, then me. She straightened. "It was so nice to see you guys, but I can't sleep knowing my friend's in trouble. I'll give you a call in a couple of days and let you know how I'm going. I'll be in Paris for the next show, but between now and then, I'm going to talk to a few of our mutual friends, see if I can fathom anything out. I'll talk to you soon."

As Sarah walked to the clear area near the door, Will opened his mouth to speak, but before he could say anything, she'd made her doorway and was gone. He sat back in the chair and slapped his hand on the couch next to him. "Damn!"

I gently grabbed his bicep. "She'll be okay. She's only going to chat to some of her friends. Let's just wait a couple of days, like she said. Maybe we can go check on her when she's in Paris, just keep tabs, make sure she isn't getting into any trouble."

Will raised a brow. "This coming from you? Normally you're the one who needs keeping tabs on. The shoe's on the other foot." He probably thought this would stop me doing my own thing in the future. Yeah, nah.

"At least I understand why she has to do this. And if there aren't any witches involved, she'll easily be able to look after herself. Right?" The words were coming out of my mouth, but why didn't I believe them? It might have something to do with the uneasy roiling of my stomach.

Will gave me a sceptical look, then turned to Angelica. "Oh, Lily was attacked at the café." Oh, yeah, that.

Angelica donned her poker face, ensuring everyone stayed calm. "You look fine. What happened?" I told her about it. When I finished, she nodded. "Right. Lucky we're having that meeting tomorrow night. Work has been taking all my attention, and I've been slack. Sorry, Lily. We need to get that sorted. I understand Millicent's father will be there too. When is he having another go at your tattoo?"

"I don't know. He wanted to do some research first, and he and his wife had a week in Spain as well. I didn't want to push since he's doing me a favour." I hated being a bother, and dismantling the tattoo was dangerous. Millicent's dad risked both of us every time he worked on it. That was a lot of pressure, and if he died because of me, I'd never forgive myself. But on the other hand, tonight had proven the tattoo was a liability. What if causing pain was the least of what they could do with it? "Oh, and I didn't tell you at the restaurant, Will, because I didn't want to worry you, but I actually did have my return to sender up when it happened. The tattoo must give them a direct link to hurt me." How that was possible, I didn't know. Going by his and Angelica's widened eyes, they didn't either.

Will took a deep breath—probably so he could yell. "What?! You don't keep things like that from me, ever! I don't care if you think there was a better time to tell me. This is important. I should've gotten you out of there straight away." Okay, so he wasn't quite yelling; it was more of an angry loudness.

Angelica had to have her say too, of course. "Lily, that changes everything. No more walking anywhere."

My eyes bugged out. "What? You can't! I won't be a prisoner in my own home… well, your home, again. I just can't." Truth be told, this was what I was really afraid of—it gave them another reason to stop me going anywhere or doing anything.

Angelica rolled her eyes. "Pish posh. Stop being so dramatic. Their spells can't attack you while you're here; otherwise they would have, but that's not why I don't want you to walk anywhere. I have a suspicion that they can probably only access the tattoo if they're within a certain radius from you. Maybe it's fifty feet, maybe it's two hundred, but, until we know, we aren't going to make it easy for them. You can travel places—the tracking part of the tattoo has been dismantled, so if you travel somewhere, they're not likely to know where you are, but it's easy for them to follow you if you leave your house and walk or drive somewhere. So no more leaving the house the normal way. All right?"

I heaved a humungous sigh. Thank God for that. "All right. That sounds fine." Crisis averted, again. So many avoided crises today. Was it a new record? I'd just have to send other people up to get my Costa fix, or maybe there was another Costa near a landing point I could visit. I'd have to check it out.

Will looked at me. "Lily, never do that again. Promise me. If anything crops up that you know changes things, you have to tell me as soon as you can." He took my chin in his hand, forcing me to meet his worried gaze.

"What if I can't keep it? I don't want to lie to you. Tonight, you needed to go and get Sarah. I was more worried about her than myself."

The intensity in his gaze ratcheted up a notch. "I don't care. I love Sarah—she's my sister—but if I had to choose to save someone, it would be you. You're the one for me, Lily. And as shitty as I feel about saying I'd save someone else over my own sister, you get my point. You're everything to me. Please promise."

I was stunned to silence, like a parent who'd just asked their child to do a chore and had been obeyed the first time—crazy, right? "Um… well, when you put it like that, okay. But please know that I can take care of myself. Hopefully that will be a choice you'll never have to make."

He pulled me in for a hug and squished me tight. Angelica cleared her throat. "Now that's settled, I think it's time we figure out what we're going to do about Sarah running off to investigate on her own. I can't really spare anyone, and I don't think she's in immediate danger, but a plan would be good, so we can minimise any trouble."

After a thirty-minute discussion, where Will said he'd text her and get her to agree to a phone tracker, among other things, I was exhausted. The RP attack and emotional conversations had stolen my energy. I yawned. "Time for bed. I'll see you both tomorrow."

"I'll be up in a few minutes. I have a couple of things to talk to Angelica about." He gave me a quick kiss on the lips, and I went upstairs. Thank goodness I was so tired; if not, thoughts of Sarah being at risk would have stopped me sleeping. But even though I fell asleep quickly, nightmares followed. Seemed there would be no respite. I should have known.

CHAPTER 5

The next morning, everyone else went to work as per normal, but I wasn't needed. I did a Pilates workout from YouTube, then had my coffee and breakfast. Afterwards, I read in my favourite armchair next to the fire. The weather wasn't too bad—cloudy and supposed to get to thirteen Celsius—but that was irrelevant since I couldn't go anywhere. Just after lunchtime, my phone rang. I jumped. Gah, damned heightened surprise reflex.

I took a couple of calming breaths before I answered Will's call. "Hey. And before you ask, I'm fine."

He didn't sound the least bit happy to hear it. "That's great, but that's not why I'm calling."

My heart, almost back to normal after my overreaction to the phone ringing, ramped up again. "What happened?"

"Have you heard from my sister?"

"No. Can't you get hold of her?"

"No. I've been trying since eight this morning. I've called her agent, and they haven't heard from her, but they didn't expect to. I'm one of her emergency contacts with them, so they gave me her itinerary. I think we need to go check things out."

"We, as in you and me?" I hoped that's what he'd meant.

"Yes, you and me. I know you're probably bored, and I could use a buffer when I get there. If she's just been avoiding my calls, you'll need to be the peacemaker." Did he really want me there for that, or was he more worried of what he'd do if he couldn't find her? Whatever the reason, he needed my support and maybe my magic.

"Do you know where she travelled to when she left last night?"

"Yes. She went to Mum and Dad's and stayed there, but they said she left at six this morning for her next job. Check in at her apartment in Paris would be at two. It's one here now, so she'll arrive there any time."

"Does she ever just stay at home and travel to where she has to be?" That would save a lot of money on hotels.

"Not usually. She could be needed by someone at short notice, and they know where to find her. Plus, she usually stays with another model or two, and it would be weird if they saw her go into her room, then couldn't find her. It's just easier for her to stay there. She likes staying in hotels, so there's that."

I chuckled. I loved hotels too, at least nice ones. There was nothing like sleeping in clean, crisp sheets every night and ordering room service. "Are you going to come get me?"

"Yep. Be ready in five, and bring your phone. We might need photos."

"Consider it done." I magicked my tracksuit off, and jeans, long-sleeved top, and coat on. Then I slipped my phone in my pocket and my credit card. If we found Sarah quickly, maybe Will would agree to visit some chic Paris café for coffee. A girl could hope. I didn't want to think about what would happen if we couldn't find her. Maybe she wasn't answering Will's calls because she was still upset. Surely that was it.

Will soon arrived and made a doorway for both of us. I scrunched my forehead. "How come I'm not making my own doorway? I don't want to come out in the men's toilets."

He smiled. "This time is something a little different. The PIB owns a studio apartment a few blocks from the hotel Sarah's booked into. We have a few landing spots like that around Europe to cover for the places that don't have convenient public toilets." Wow, expensive landing spots. And I supposed you couldn't live in them or rent them out, even to witches, because strangers would constantly be coming and going.

"Um, okay." I shrugged and stepped through into a small, white-tiled bathroom with shower, toilet, bidet, and single-bowl marble vanity. I didn't linger because the space wasn't super big, and Will would have bumped into me.

The apartment was one huge room with no furniture. Sunlight poured in from three tall windows facing the street. It shone across straw-coloured wooden floors and white walls. What a cosy space. Such a shame no one could live here.

Will's booted steps clomped loudly on the timber floor. He was in uniform, and his face was in serious mode. The forehead lines were on show, and his grey eyes were more stormy sea than cloudy afternoon. I bit back a sigh. He was so sexy. Was it wrong of me to notice it now, when we were looking for his sister? I guessed you couldn't help when inspiration struck.

He opened the front door, and I followed him out. He magicked the lock shut, then hurried down one flight of stairs. I made sure my return to sender was up—not that it helped against RP now.

We stepped outside. Ah, Paris, how I loved thee. It was good to be back, albeit in stressful circumstances, although that was how it usually happened. I took in the cityscape, making a note to be careful crossing the street since they were driving on the wrong side.

Within six minutes, we'd reached her hotel. La Clef Tour Eiffel Paris was in a gorgeous seven-storey nineteenth-century building. We crossed the road. Will stopped on the footpath outside and turned to me. "No-notice spell, please. Just stand near the lift while you're waiting for me. I'm going to get her room number." I wasn't going to ask how. Witches weren't allowed to coerce information out of others, unless they had special permission from the PIB, and I was pretty sure Will hadn't gotten any. Maybe he was going to charm the information out of them? In any case, I wasn't going to ask. We needed to know, and it wasn't like we were stalkers or anything.

I activated my spell. "Done."

He turned and led the way inside the elegant double-height arched entry. Talk about luxury. Another reminder of how well the modelling thing paid. I traversed the stone-tiled floor to the lift and waited. I grabbed my phone out of my coat pocket and texted Sarah. *We're in Paris at your hotel. Are you around?*

It took Will a few minutes to join me. He wore a poker face, so I had no idea if he'd succeeded. "Well?" I asked. He gave a small nod, but none of the tension leached out of me—my text had gone unanswered. I didn't see the point of telling Will—he'd already tried with no success several times. One more wasn't going to be a surprise. "Did she check in?"

"No. Her friend did."

"Then why are we going up? We can't just barge in on a stranger."

He raised a brow. "I'm not stupid, Lily. Give me a little credit. We'll knock and explain we're worried about her. Maybe her friend can provide some information. If she's not there, we'll use the key. Who knows, maybe her friend checked in, and Sarah went straight to the room?"

Something else hit me. "How come you even needed a key? You locked the other unit with magic. Can't you just unlock any door with magic?"

"Yes, but I don't want to leave a magic signature behind. First lesson of being an agent is leave as little evidence behind as possible. We're basically undercover. We don't know whether anything has happened to Sarah, but if something has and a witch is behind it, we don't want them knowing that we're onto them."

"Right, okay. That sort of makes sense, but it seems like a lot of work for nothing." He frowned. I put my hands up. "It's fine. We're doing it your way, Agent Crankypants. I was just giving you my thoughts."

The lift opened, ending our conversation, and a middle-aged couple got out. We slipped into the elevator, and Will pressed the button for the fourth floor. Up we went. When the lift stopped, Will wasted no time and hurried out and along the hallway. At the hotel-room door, he paused. I looked at him. "What are you doing?"

After a moment, he whispered, "Just making sure there's no one doing any magic." He was overreacting. I wasn't going to say anything though. If Sarah wasn't here, there was no reason for all this secrecy. If, God forbid, something had happened to her, it wouldn't have happened here, which meant there'd be no evidence.

Will knocked. It didn't take long for someone to answer… and it wasn't a statuesque model, as we both expected. He was statuesque, but he wasn't any kind of model I'd ever seen. The man in front of us was about Will's height but slimmer, less muscly. He looked to be half Asian, half European, with olive skin, dark eyes, a petite nose, and short, purple hair. He wore a cream-coloured angora sweater, the deep vee showing off his hairless chest. His full lips—which looked to have had some filler recently—were deep purple. Fake lashes and eyeliner framed his eyes. He placed one hand on his hip and looked Will up and down in a playful way. He smiled. "I hope I can help you." I suppressed a giggle.

Will didn't miss a beat. He gave him a friendly smile and held out his hand. "I'm Will, Sarah's brother. I was wondering if my sister was here yet. She asked me to come visit when she arrived."

The purple-haired man shook his hand. "Lovely to meet you! I'm Lavender. I'm a make-up artist booked for the same show as Sarah. She's one of my besties in the circus." Circus? I was about to ask a truly dumb question, when he looked at me and chuckled. "No, darling, not the actual circus. I call this fashion thing the circus because, really, it's colourful, crazy, and full of performers, and a lion or two, if you get my drift. And what's your name, sweetie?"

I smiled—his open, friendly manner put me at ease. "I'm Lily, Will's girlfriend." I held out my hand, and he shook it.

"Welcome to our Paris abode. Sarah's not here yet, but please come in." Lavender turned and made his way to a fawn-coloured fabric couch. Will sat next to him, and I sat in the red armchair opposite. It must be an apartment-style room. There were three doors off the living area—likely two bedrooms and a guest toilet.

The main room had these couches, a four-seat dining table, and a large TV on one wall. It contained all manner of designer lamps, cushions, framed prints on the walls, and a rug. Not too shabby.

"Can I get you anything to drink?"

Will smiled. "No thanks. Do you have any idea when Sarah will be back?"

"She hasn't arrived yet, which is odd. She's usually the first one to check in." He reached into his jeans pocket and pulled out his phone. He looked at the screen and pouted. "Naughty Sarah hasn't left a message. She's usually very good about communicating." He looked up at me and narrowed his eyes. Uh-oh. "Did Sarah really ask you to come here, or is she avoiding you?"

This guy was good. Before I could stop myself, my eyes widened. Crap. Where was my poker face when I needed it? Will rolled his eyes, then shook his head. "I wouldn't say she's avoiding us. We had a slight disagreement yesterday, but that's why we're here. We're just worried about her. I've been trying to get in touch, and she won't answer."

Lavender stood. "I'm sorry, but I'm going to have to ask you to leave. I will tell Sarah you passed by, but if she doesn't want to see you, I have to protect her wishes." I wasn't sure how he'd make us leave if Will didn't want to—he didn't look nearly as strong as Will. I checked him out with my other sight. Oh, he was a witch. I was pretty sure Will wouldn't want to get into a magical stoush. Ma'am would be sure to find out, and there'd be hell to pay.

This was my fault. I really should try and fix it. I stood. "Look, we're not here to cause trouble, but we really are worried about her. Do you know her friend Luisa?" Will jumped to his feet and gave me a strained shut-up look. It wasn't as if this guy could have been involved, could he? He seemed too nice.

Will schooled his face to poker setting and looked at Lavender. "Look, Luisa is missing, and we're worried someone could be targeting her friends too. You said yourself that Sarah is always first to check in, and she hasn't messaged you. Have you sent her one?" So he was trying to get information without giving him the full story. I guessed it was the sensible thing to do just in case this guy was the culprit.

Lavender folded his arms, thumbs tucked in but leaving his fingers splayed on his upper arms. He flapped the fingers of one hand against his upper arm but didn't say a word. The rhythmic slapping echoed in the quiet room. *Slap, slap, slap, slap, slap, slap*. It was like a form of water torture. Was he going to do that all day and wait for us to be annoyed enough to leave? He kept going while he stared Will down. I sighed.

It was time to intervene. "For crying out loud. Aren't you worried about her? You're not much of a friend, wasting time while she could be in danger." I knew Will would be angry at what I was going to do next, but stuff it. Might as well get Lavender's reaction, and if he wasn't the bad guy, he'd be more likely to help. I opened my eyes wide and sucked in a sharp breath. "Or are *you* the bad guy? What have you done with her?" I ran to one of the doors. "Is she in here?" I flung open the door to an empty bedroom; then I went to the next one and opened that too, revealing a bed with a suitcase on the top of it—Lavender obviously hadn't had a chance to unpack yet.

Lavender sighed dramatically. "Fine. I did text her, and I haven't heard anything back. I am not the bad guy here, and I have been worried about her. This whole thing with Luisa is very strange. She's not the type to steal anything, let alone millions of pounds' worth of jewellery."

"Do you mind if I cast a truth spell on you?" Will asked. Wow, that was bold. The average witch wouldn't know how to do that, and the PIB agents who were talented enough to do it were only allowed to use it in extreme circumstances if they didn't have someone's permission. Only an innocent person would allow that.

Lavender hesitated. "Who are you?"

"I told you; I'm Sarah's brother."

"You know what I'm asking." He waved a flamboyant hand towards Will. "What do you do in the real world? Who is Will Blakesley when he's at work?"

It wasn't like it was a secret to be an agent in the PIB, except if you were working undercover, which he did at times. Maybe he wanted to be discrete. I would think his sister's safety came before his secrecy in this case. Maybe he could tell him, then cast a forget spell, although they were risky too.

Will locked eyes with me. I was going to shrug, but he was looking for my opinion. What was my gut feeling on this guy? I glanced at Lavender, then back at Will. I nodded. Will turned back to Lavender. "I'm a PIB agent—don't go spreading it around. My job is to keep people safe, and I have a feeling about Sarah and this whole situation. So, are you going to help us or not?" Will stared at Lavender. Lavender glared back. Then, finally, Lavender gave in, and I slowly let out my breath.

"Fine. I'll help you, but if you do wrong by me or your sister, things will get ugly… very ugly. I spent part of my teens on the streets, and I know how to cut a witch."

Wow, Lavender wasn't nearly as delicate or joyful as his name and hair colour suggested. Will wasn't fazed, if his bemused expression was anything to go by.

Will held his hand out. Lavender shook it firmly. "You get to ask one question only under the truth spell. Make it a good one."

Will nodded. "Fair enough. Ready?" Lavender nodded. Will's magic tingled my scalp as he verbalised the spell. "The question I'm about to ask will be answered in truth, lest all further spells Lavender casts will fail in their task." Lavender's eyes bugged wide—those were pretty harsh terms. "Lavender, have you done anything to harm my sister?"

His face contorted as his lips answered what his brain didn't want. "Y-Yes." He slammed his hand over his mouth.

Will's mouth dropped open—he obviously hadn't been expecting that answer either. Once he wrangled the surprise off his face, thunderclouds moved in, and he stepped forward, his face millimetres from Lavender's. "What did you do? So help me—"

The make-up artist held up his hand. "No, no, it's nothing like that. She asked me to bleach her hair once, and I stuffed up—I'm not a hairdresser, you know. It all fell out. She had to wear a wig for six months until her hair was long enough to take hair extensions. It was a real disaster. You have no idea."

Will's brow furrowed. "And that's it? You've never hurt her?"

Lavender rolled his eyes. "Of course not. She's one of my best friends. I love Sarah. If someone has hurt her, they'll have to answer to me." His glare was fierce. "Are we good?"

Will nodded. "Yes, we're good. Do you think you can try and call her?"

Lavender nodded and pulled his phone out of his pocket. He tapped the screen a few times and put the phone on speaker. The call went straight to voicemail. Damn. "This is

Sarah. Please leave a message after the beep, and I'll get back to you as soon as I can." *Beep*.

"Hello, lovely. This is your favourite make-up artist extraordinaire. Call me, hon. It's urgent." He hung up, and we all looked at each other, worry evident in everyone's eyes. Lavender looked at Will. "How do we proceed? Do we give her time to get back to me, or do you want to do something now?"

Will blew out a breath and ran a hand through his hair. "She left my parents' early this morning, so she hasn't been gone long enough to be officially missing, at least not without any extenuating circumstances like someone threatening her. Can we sit down again? I'd like to ask you about your shared contacts."

"Of course." Lavender fell into the couch and pulled an orange handkerchief out of his pocket to dab at his forehead. "If anything happens to her…."

I sat on the armchair again. "I know, but we'll do whatever we can to make sure she's okay. Will's the best at what he does." I gave a half smile and tried to hide the misgivings fizzing in my stomach like a sherbet bomb. What if she'd figured out who hurt her friend and went to confront them? Surely she would've come to us first? I sagged lower in the chair. Maybe she wanted to but decided against it because of how Will had reacted last time?

Will sat next to Lavender. "Do you think Luisa took the jewels?"

He shook his head firmly. "Definitely not."

"Do you have any theories on who did?" Will leaned forward slightly. He obviously wasn't going to tell him that we knew she'd taken them—there was no way to explain how we knew. Maybe Sarah stumbled onto her friend and realised she had stolen the jewels. Crap.

Lavender rubbed his hands up and down his thighs while he thought. "I don't like to make assumptions, but let's just say that more than one person thinks it was Evelyn. I'm assuming, if you've looked into this even a little bit, that you know who she is."

Will nodded. "The only problem is that she hasn't disappeared, her place has been searched, and nothing was found. She's off the hook as far as the police are concerned."

"I'm sure there would've been at least one or two gold diggers there. Although I'm not sure any of them would bother stealing anything. They can very well get what they want by batting their eyelashes and showing some flesh." That was not helpful. He didn't have any ideas that would break this case wide open.

I licked my bottom lip and hoped Will didn't think my idea was stupid. "Why don't we visit Luisa's home? What if Sarah went to see her, managed to find her, and realised she was guilty? If her friend was capable of stealing the jewels, what's to stop her being capable of hurting Sarah?"

The tightness around Will's eyes indicated he thought it was rather likely.

Lavender pressed his lips together and shook his head. "I just can't believe Weezie would do that. But if you want to cross it off your list, why don't we just go? I have her address. I've been to her place a few times."

"Does she know about witches?" Will asked.

"No, and I have no idea why not. Her ex was one, as are two of her best friends, but I've never said anything, neither has Sarah, and Weezie has never brought it up. I just have to assume her ex never said anything."

"Okay. Let's get this done." Will stood. "Where's the nearest landing spot?"

"The toilets at the train station in Florence, or Firenze, as the locals call it."

Will nodded. "Do you know how to make a no-notice spell?"

Lavender's well-groomed eyebrows scrunched down. "A what?"

"It's kind of a law-enforcement thing. It stops non-witches noticing you. You're not exactly invisible, but you'll be ignored unless you crash into someone."

Lavender nodded slowly. "Sweetie, going unnoticed is the last thing I usually want." He laughed. "But it does sound really cool for bad-hair days. Can you show me?"

Will told him how to do it and watched while he put it in place. "Great. Now can you send the station coordinates to me and Lily?"

Lavender nodded. "Stand by." The golden numbers popped into my head. How did everyone know how to witch, yet I had no idea? Maybe their parents showed them all this stuff when they came of age, or even before, in readiness? The shadow of my old companion Melancholy cast darkness around me for a moment. I made my doorway and stepped away from Mr Melancholy into an echoey public toilet. Nothing like entering a public toilet to shift your focus. I came out of the cubicle and realised why we needed no-notice spells. A tall, middle-aged woman, her dark hair in a bun, had her back to me, collecting money from another woman who needed to use the toilet. Gah, paid toilets. In Australia, all public toilets were free, and I still couldn't get used to the user-pays system.

I snuck past her, turning to the side and sucking my

stomach in. I opened the door and hurried out. She must have thought the door opening was weird, but it was too late for me to do anything about it—I was out on the concourse, and I doubted she'd chase me. It took a few seconds for me to find Will and Lavender in the crowded station.

Once we were reunited, we dropped our no-notice spells, and Lavender took the lead. I hurried behind with Will. "Have you ever been to Florence before?" I asked him.

"Yes." I'd been hoping for more information than that, like how many times, did he know it well, etcetera. But I supposed he was stressed about Sarah, and now was not the time to chat. I'd never been before, so when we exited into the street, I greedily took in everything around me.

Lavender headed for the taxi rank and hopped in the nearest one. He sat in the front while Will and I slid into the back. Lavender instructed the driver, "Via Odorico da Pordenone, grazie." Ooh, he knew some Italian. I supposed those in the modelling industry travelled a lot, and it was only normal they would be multilingual. Hmm, maybe I should learn some languages in my spare time. Goodness knew I found myself home alone enough, thanks to stupid RP, that I could probably become fluent in at least two more languages in a year.

Will stared out the window for the whole trip, and so did I. No one was in the mood to talk. We eventually turned into a one-way street, and the driver asked something in Italian. Lavender responded, and I had no idea what the hell they were talking about. We drove halfway down the street, and the taxi stopped. "I've got this," said Will. He handed his credit card to the driver. Once the payment was done, we all hopped out and re-donned our no notices.

Lavender led us to the security entrance of a multi-level 1970s unit block. Not the most attractive building I'd ever seen, but it seemed to be the norm in this area. Where France was all prettiness and well-kept character, and England was all charm and quaintness, Italy seemed to be the take-me-as-I-am aunt. Everything was a bit dirtier and less well kept. Some buildings had flaking paint, and there weren't as many green spaces, not to mention a lot of the development was twentieth century rather than eighteenth or nineteenth. Tiny cars and Vespas zipped around the streets and parked on corners when there was nowhere else to park. There was a liveliness about it though, and even a sense of history, different but no less enchanting than France and England—I loved anything different than what I was used to, provided I felt safe, which I did.

Will stood back from the front entrance for a moment and whispered to me. "Can you take some photos? Ask if Sarah's been here in the last twenty-four hours?" I nodded.

Lavender, who'd magicked open the security door after buzzing Luisa's apartment and getting no answer, narrowed his eyes at us. "What are you whispering about?"

"Nothing much." Will's bland expression shouted that he wasn't going to say anything else.

Lavender shook his head. "Well, are you coming, or not?"

I gave Will a small push and said quietly, "I'll get them in the hallway." I figured if I couldn't get any pictures of her inside the building, I'd then try outside.

We trudged up two flights of stairs. While Lavender knocked on the door, I surreptitiously meandered a few steps down the hallway and turned so I was facing him. I didn't draw on the river of power, just my internal source, to avoid alerting Lavender to the fact I was using magic. I thought to the universe, or whatever controlled my magic, *Show me Sarah here in the last twenty-four hours*.

Lavender knocked louder, but in my shot, he wasn't standing there; Sarah was, hand raised, her knuckles about to make contact with the door. I snapped just one picture—that was all we needed. *Show me if the door opened for Sarah.* The scene changed, and there she was, stepping through an open door. Adrenaline shot through me, and my stomach dropped, as if I was on a rollercoaster. Was she still inside?

I stepped closer to the door to see who had let her in, or had she let herself in?

The only person in the frame was Will's sister, so either she'd let herself in or someone was behind the door. The only way to find out was to take a photo inside. I clicked a shot so Will could see.

"What are you doing?"

Crap.

I looked up from the phone screen. Lavender was staring at me. "Just taking a photo for later. Will might want to go through the scene if it turns out Sarah has been here."

"Let me see."

Double crap. I swallowed. "I haven't taken anything yet. Hang on a sec." I held the phone up and clicked a few shots of Lavender in front of the door, then turned and took some shots of the hallway, hoping I had enough that if he scrolled, he wouldn't get to the one of Sarah because that was something I could never explain. I put the phone in front of him and showed him. I scrolled through about five photos, then clicked the screen off and slid the phone in my pocket. "See, just harmless photos of the scene."

"I like to record everything about a crime scene. It's a habit that often comes in handy." Will stepped towards the doorway. "Let's not touch anything when we're inside."

"Do you want me to magic it open?" the make-up artist asked.

"I don't want to leave evidence behind, but I'm sure the police have already checked the place, and the PIB isn't on the case anymore, so we should be safe."

"Maybe you should do it." Lavender stepped back from the doorway.

"I could, but it would be better if you did it. You have an excuse—you're a friend checking up on a friend. Have you ever been arrested before?"

His brow furrowed. "No, why?"

"Then your magic signature won't be on file, but mine will. The PIB takes a record of every agent's magic profile. Look, if anything happens, I'll vouch for you. Okay?"

Lavender looked from Will to me and back again, twirling the diamond stud in one ear as he did. "Time for reciprocation. I want you to spell a promise."

Without hesitation, Will nodded. He was a man of his word, so promising this was not a big deal. His magic feathered my scalp, and I shivered. "I, Will Blakesley, on threat of losing the pinkie finger of my left hand, promise to defend Lavender's character and do everything I can to stop any legal or otherwise harm from coming to him if this goes wrong."

A bell tinkled, and Lavender nodded. "Thank you, Will."

"My pleasure."

I was sure I'd heard that bell a few months ago, and had probably asked the question about it, but I couldn't quite remember. "Was that bell a sign the promise has been recorded?"

Will answered, "Yes."

"So, it's not for an angel getting its wings?" Will just looked at me, totally unimpressed. Yep, his sense of humour had definitely left for the day. I sighed. "Never mind." At least Lavender smirked, his eyes twinkling with mirth. I smiled in thanks. You could never surround yourself with too many people who thought you were funny. He must be a keeper. Hopefully Sarah wouldn't mind sharing him. My smile faded. She'd better be okay, dammit.

Lavender put his hand near the door and mumbled something. His magic signature was light and airy, peaceful. He was a good person if his magic was anything to go by. I got an impression of witches' personalities from their magic, but I never considered how accurate my impressions were. Was it another way I could vet people, or at least figure out what they were like? Something to consider for later.

When the door swung open, Will was so close behind Lavender that he was almost pushing him through the door. I stood back and let them enter first. Tension clenched my jaw, and my neck ached. *Please don't find anything bad.* Once the guys were inside and I'd allowed enough time for a reaction that didn't happen, I went in.

The apartment had an open-plan living area with lime-washed timber floors and white walls. It was decorated in a shabby chic style—very feminine and pretty with muted pastel upholstery and distressed white timber tables. There was a bit of mess—a blue throw rug piled on the floor, papers spread across the dining table, and an item of clothing on one of the couches. I wrinkled my nose. Someone needed to take out the garbage.

"She obviously hasn't been here for a while. That bin stinks." I made my way to the kitchen, which was separated from the living area by a large island bench. My nose led me straight to the cupboard hiding the garbage. When I opened the door, the odour jumped me. Yep, it's definitely that. I slammed the door and coughed into my arm. Ew. Gross.

There were three doors off the living room. The men had gone into one each—likely bedrooms and a bathroom. While Lavender wasn't watching, I whipped out my phone and pulled up the camera app. "Show me if Sarah was here in the last twenty-four hours."

There she was, standing next to the dining table, not touching anything, but looking at the papers upon it. I took a couple of shots, then walked up to the table to look at what the papers were. Hmm, they were all in Italian. Some of them must've been bills because they had euro amounts at the bottom. The rest of the paperwork was beyond my Italian skills because I didn't know anything other than *ciao*, *si*, and *Buongiorno*, oh, and cappuccino. How could I forget that one?

I held the phone up again. I whispered the next instruction, nausea washing up my throat as I did. "Show me Sarah hurt or… killed." I held my breath and looked at the screen.

Thank God. The screen showed me the apartment as it was right now.

I sucked in a breath and hung my head in relief.

"Lily, are you all right?" Will rushed over.

I looked up. "Yes, yes, I'm fine. Just relieved. I'll tell you later." I lowered my voice. "She was here."

His eyes bugged open, and he grabbed my upper arm. "I need some fresh air." He opened the balcony door, took me outside, and shut the door. "Show me." I handed him the phone, and he flicked through the photos.

"I asked to see her hurt or… dead. Nothing showed up." His gaze met mine, and the relief in his eyes flowed over me. I gave him a hug. "I know this is tough, but we'll find her alive and well."

He wrapped one arm around me and rested his cheek against my head. "I hope so, Lily. I bloody well hope so." He straightened and handed me my phone. "The question is, what did she find, and where did she go next?"

There was a sharp rap on the glass, and I jumped. Lavender. I slid the door open. "Thanks for the heart attack. I really hate when the day goes by and I miss out."

He smirked. "Sorry, sweetie. You need something to relax you. You're too highly strung."

"Yeah, you should probably cut down on the coffee." Will's poker face was back. I was sure he was joking… wasn't he?

I was half joshing when I said, "What? Are you mad? How can you ask me to give up the one thing that makes me truly happy?"

His eyes widened. "What do you mean? Don't I make you happy?" His face was aghast.

I laughed. "Of course you do, but don't mess with my other addiction. I'd be really lonely if it were just me and my coffee." I knew this wasn't the best time for humour, but we needed to keep our spirits up. If we could stay somewhat calm about this, we'd be less likely to make mistakes or miss things.

Lavender chuckled. "It's like that, is it? Poor Will." He patted Will's shoulder. "I'll be your shoulder to cry on if she ever makes that choice. Don't worry." He winked, and Will leaned back slightly. I tried not to giggle—Lavender was likely teasing him. Before Will stroked out trying to figure what the deal was, Lavender shook his head. "Don't worry. You're safe. I'm just pulling your chain."

Will smiled. "Thanks. I'm not into guys, but if I ever change my mind, you'll be the first guy I call." Okay, *now* it was getting weird. "But, seriously, I need to ask a favour."

Lavender nodded. "Shoot."

"That paperwork on the table, can you have a squiz and tell me if there's anything there that would have made Sarah look somewhere else for Luisa?"

"Okay. But how do you know she was even here?"

"Let's just assume."

I put up my hand. "Um, question."

"Yes, Lily, and put your hand down. Ma'am's not here." The corner of Will's mouth quirked up.

I lowered my hand. "Sorry. Just wanted to get your attention. How could Sarah read all that stuff? Can she speak Italian?"

Will smiled his proud, brotherly smile. "That's her talent. She can spell languages into her brain. She's fluent in any language she wants to be. It takes her about a month of embedding to learn a new language, but once she does, it's hers for life, as good as a native speaker. I'm pretty sure she knows French, German, Mandarin, Swedish, Italian, Spanish, and Greek. For all I know, there's more."

My mouth dropped open. "Wow, impressive." What a cool talent to have. It was a shame you couldn't swap one talent for another. I'd gladly swap being able to tell the differences between people's magic for that one.

While I'd been thinking about stupid stuff, Lavender went inside, and Will followed. Just inside, he turned, his forehead wrinkled, and his eyes radiating concern. "Come on, Lily. We're wasting time." He had a very good point. I was doing my best to believe Sarah was fine, maybe just ignoring us, but the longer she didn't even get back to Lavender, the worse it was looking. She could be on the brink of life and death, and we were the only ones looking for her. We really did need to work faster.

While they scoured the paperwork, I wandered into both

bedrooms and the bathroom and asked if Luisa had been here since the fashion show. Nothing. I subtly held my camera up and scanned the living room area from the bathroom doorway. Still nothing. She hadn't returned since that night. Interesting. Not only that, but her wardrobe and chest of drawers were full of clothes.

I called out from my position at the bathroom door. "Will, do you know if Luisa's used any of her bank accounts? Surely the PIB checked that out straight away."

"They had checked, and no, she hadn't accessed any money. We should probably try and update that information too. Maybe she's accessed her credit card or account today?"

I shook my head. "Why would you give yourself away like that if you'd stolen stuff? There's no way she'll use it. Besides, if she sells the jewellery, she'll have cash and maybe a new bank account to put it in under a false name."

Lavender looked at me and pressed his lips together. I knew he didn't believe she'd done it, but he stayed silent. And I couldn't say anything because my proof was a secret. Time to move on. I walked to the table. "Did you find anything useful?"

Lavender twirled the small diamond stud in his ear. "A few bills, but nothing exorbitant. Wouldn't the police have gone through this already and taken anything of note?"

"Yes," said Will, "but you never know what they missed. They'd also have her bank account and credit-card statements electronically. It's worth going through that pile, just in case."

Lavender, his hands covered by his sleeves so he didn't leave fingerprints, finished rummaging. Unfortunately, his hands were empty.

"Nothing?" I asked.

"Nope, nothing. Now what?" I didn't have an answer to his

question, so I looked at the person who would. Will.

He pulled out his phone. "I'd like to look through her credit-card statements. Hang on a moment." He dialled someone and put the phone to his ear. "Hey, can you do me a favour?" He turned and looked out the window, then chuckled. "Very funny." His voice turned serious. "Sarah's missing.... Yeah, I know.... I'll explain later. I'm just with your sister and one of Sarah's friends trying to figure it out. I just need access to her credit-card and bank statements. Do you think you could send them to me?" He waited a moment. "Okay, yeah, great. Ready and waiting, and, yeah, maybe don't tell anyone. Thanks. Bye."

"You didn't want to get Ma'am in trouble?" Calling my brother was a good move—he wasn't under as much scrutiny as Ma'am, and he would do anything to help his mates.

"No. And if anyone found out she'd sent me documents from a case we weren't investigating, she could get into a lot of trouble for breaking confidentiality codes. Plus, the last thing I need is for Chad to call me in just to annoy Ma'am. I need to find my sister, and the PIB wouldn't consider this as something to investigate since she's only been out of touch for a few hours." Will's phoned dinged. He opened an app. "He's emailed them. I don't want to leave any evidence here, so I think we should continue this back at our place."

"Where's that?" asked Lavender.

Will answered, "Westerham. Do you think you can make a doorway for all of us to travel through?"

"I can handle that. Is that so you don't leave your magic signatures here?"

Will gave him an apologetic look. "Yes. Sorry. Look, the PIB isn't even investigating at this stage, and it should fade within a few days. We can travel from the downstairs hallway if you like. We can reactivate our no-notice spells, just in case anyone is looking out of their peephole. Chances are, we won't be noticed or seen, and if anyone did notice, they'd think they were crazy." That wasn't exactly nice, but he was right. We didn't want to waste time catching a taxi back to the train station to disappear from the privacy of their toilets.

Lavender sighed. "Fine. Come on." He opened the front door, then wiped it of all fingerprints. After he shut it, he wiped any prints of that, then locked it with magic. We followed him downstairs, and, after checking no one was around, Will sent him the coordinates to Angelica's reception room. Within thirty seconds, we were home.

"Thanks, Lav," I said. Hmm, hopefully he didn't mind me shortening his name. At least I didn't call him Lavo—the normal Aussie thing was to shorten and add an o, like Johnno, smoko, and Danno, but he probably wouldn't get it, and then I'd have to explain. Was it lazy of me to find having to explain tiring?

Will unlocked the reception-room door and made his way to the kitchen. A subtle touch of his magic on my nape and some whispered words, and a pile of paper appeared in his hand. "Here are the statements." He drew more magic. Three highlighters appeared in his other hand. He divided the papers among the three of us and handed us each a highlighter. He sat. "Highlight any large or weird purchases—don't worry about groceries, petrol, electricity bills, anything ordinary. We're looking for stuff that isn't a regular thing."

I sat next to him, and Lav sat at the head of the table. We got to work. After about fifteen minutes, Will's phone rang. He snatched it out of his pocket, but when he saw who it was, his face fell. Obviously not Sarah. My shoulders sagged. So disappointing. "Hello, Ma'am. Yes. Okay. I'll be there in five." Will hung up. "I have to go into work, but I'll try and be back as soon as I can. If you find anything, let me know." He divided up the papers he hadn't been through and handed us half each. He stood and kissed the top of my head. "Thanks, guys. I really appreciate it." Before we could acknowledge him, he made his doorway and left.

"Looks like it's just you and me, kid." Lavender winked.

I chuckled. "At least I have company this time. Normally everyone runs off and leaves me. I'd just like to point out that Sarah has good taste in friends."

He grinned. "I've always said she was smart." His smile fell. "On a more serious note, she's one of the most reliable people I know. I didn't want to worry her brother more than he already is, but this gives me the heebie-jeebies. This is so out of character for her." Concern radiated from his dark eyes.

"I know. I'm trying not to think the worst. We'll just have to work faster and come up with some way to find her."

"Agreed." With that, we both put our heads down and scanned the bank statements. After a few minutes, I'd only highlighted a couple of large payments, but Lav looked up. "Hey, I might have something here. There's two payments of over four thousand euros each." He showed me his statement.

"Cassina is the first one, for four thousand eight hundred. That's a high-end furniture store. The other one is for Gucci. That's four thousand two fifty."

"Should we go back to her place and check whether she had any of that furniture?"

He shook his head. "Everything we saw there was there at least a year ago, and this statement is from November."

"So she bought furniture for someone else. Maybe her parents?"

"We need to find out."

"What's the significance of Gucci? She's a model; doesn't she usually buy designer brands?" I had no idea about these kinds of things, being someone who was lucky if she spent a hundred pounds on a piece of clothing. I couldn't imagine going on a shopping spree and dropping over four thousand euros. That was just crazy.

He looked around, as if he were about to tell me a secret. He whispered, "Don't tell anyone, but she doesn't like to wear Gucci." He sat up straight and spoke at a normal level. "If anyone asks a model about a brand, they will profess to love it. It's their job to act like they love every brand. I mean, would you hire someone to model for you if they said they didn't like your clothes? I think not. Anyway, this is a red flag. I couldn't see her buying someone this for a present either. She's not into splashing money around for fun, at least not that amount."

"Okay, well, taking into account everything you said, the two things I found might be relevant, unless they were a Christmas present to herself or her mother." I slid my piece of paper to him.

He scanned the highlighted amounts, and his eyes widened. He took in a shocked breath and daintily covered his mouth with his palm. He looked at me. "This… this from Givenchy. It's for three thousand euros. She wanted one of their handbags for everyday stuff, and I know if she'd bought it for herself, it would have been the first thing she would have shown me as soon as she'd seen me. She was saving up for one. This doesn't make sense."

"Could she have bought it for her mother?"

"We'll have to check." He looked down at the statement again. "Holy mother of hairless yappy dogs! This is crazy." I had no doubt he was talking about the fifteen-thousand-euro amount to Rolex. "She doesn't wear a watch. Her father's a down-to-earth man—he would never accept a gift like this. She was saving to help them renovate their house because it's rather dated. I can't see her spending this kind of money on something so, so—well, she would say unnecessary. I love the finer things, sweetie, but I'm looking at it from her point of view."

I smirked. "Of course. So you wouldn't say no to a new Rolex?"

His eyes lit up. "Why? Have you got one for me?"

"Yeah, nah." I smiled at his feigned disappointment. "So, what do you make of it? Do you think someone's blackmailing her, or maybe someone conned her, and that's why she took the jewellery—so she could meet her debts?"

He fiddled with his diamond stud. "I don't know. Could be either; could be neither."

"That's not super helpful." I raised a brow and folded my arms, for a moment feeling very Ma'amish. I guessed some of her haughtiness was bound to rub off on me eventually.

He rolled his eyes. "Well, sweetie, I'm sorry, but I'm a make-up artist, not a secret agent."

"No need to get testy, Mr Make-Up Artist." I raised both brows this time.

He sighed. "Argh, I'm sorry I'm not being much help. Maybe I just need more thinking time? This is all new to me."

"Sorry. I guess I'm stressed too. I'm not normally so… difficult."

He waved my comment away. "No problemo. You know what?"

"What?"

"I always think better with a margarita in my hand." A martini glass with pale-yellow icy liquid popped into his hand. A slice of lime was wedged on the side of the glass, and a sparkly blue straw stuck out of it. He took a sip. "Mmm. Would you like one?"

"Um, no thanks. I'll probably fall asleep if I have any alcohol. I could go a cappuccino though." I drew a trickle of magic, and a frothy, chocolate-topped coffee appeared on the table. Sometimes I really loved being a witch. I held up my cup for a toast. "To solving this mystery ASAP."

"Here, here." He raised his glass and clinked it against my cup. "I think we really need to visit her parents. They might have some answers. They should be able to tell us whether she bought any of those things for herself or them. At least that's a starting point."

"Agreed. And we have nothing else, so it's definitely better than doing nothing."

"So, you want to come with me?"

Oh, dear. How to explain that I was housebound unless I had protection, or how not to explain while not sounding like a weirdo.... "I don't think we should go unless we let Will know. He might have stuff he wants to ask, and if he misses his opportunity to tell you what he needs, I'll get in trouble."

His well-groomed eyebrows drew down. "What do you mean trouble? He doesn't hurt you, does he?"

My mouth dropped open. "Oh my goodness, no! Will would never hurt anyone... at least anyone who isn't a criminal trying to escape." I laughed. "I just mean, he'll be cranky and super annoying. You don't want me to have to put up with that, do you?"

He chuckled. "No, sweetie. Definitely not. Right, well, I'll finish this bev, and you can call him, let him know what we think."

I dialled Will, but he didn't answer. I left a message with no real details—you never knew who was listening in. "Right.

We'll give him twenty minutes to get back to us, and if he doesn't, there is someone else I can call who works with him. Maybe they can help."

"Help? You weren't going to do anything but stand in the bushes, as I recall."

I grinned. He had a funny idea about being an agent—not that I was one. "Bushes? Staying out of sight at a café is hardly hiding in foliage. I just think having someone else with us in place of Will might be a good idea. He won't complain as much if someone else is there to make sure we investigate properly."

"Fair enough. Let's keep going through these while we wait." He drained his drink and magicked the glass away.

By the time the twenty minutes were up, we'd found another three suspicious transactions going back to September last year. We checked through the previous months, all the way back to January, but there wasn't anything else. Hmm… "What changed for her in September? Can you remember anything? Did she get more jobs, or did she have more stress that made her spend out of her comfort zone?" People didn't just change for no reason.

"There might be something. Just a moment." He pulled out his phone and went into his message app. After a few minutes of scrolling and reading, he nodded to himself, and said, "Aha! Thought so." Then he twirled the stud in his ear and gave a smug smile. Seriously, he wasn't just going to tell me?

"Hello, Mr Make-up Artist. Want to share?" Patience was not high on my list of skills, especially when someone I cared about was in trouble.

"Sorry, I was busy congratulating myself on my brilliance. She broke up with her boyfriend in August, or, rather, she said it was mutual, but she was upset. As much as she wanted to leave him because he was too controlling, he agreed to the split. He'd done a number on her self-esteem while they'd been together, so maybe she's spending to make herself feel better?" Then he sighed. "But that just doesn't feel right. I've known her for three years, and she's never done that before, even with her previous break-ups. Anyway, I do know that whatever this is started just after her break-up."

"Okay, at least we have *something*." Getting closer to a reason would mean we could decipher a motive, but did that mean we'd figure out where she was and where Sarah was? There had to be something more to it though. Sarah was a witch, and Luisa wasn't. It would be almost impossible for Luisa to kidnap or hurt her, unless she pulled a weapon on her without warning. Still, that didn't sound likely. Gah, I hated having no answers.

"Are you going to call your backup?"

"Yes, okay." Will probably still wouldn't be happy, but he would want us to do something to get Sarah back sooner rather than later. What if he was tied up until late tonight? Knowing the PIB, that wouldn't be out of the question. I pulled up Imani's number and pressed dial. When she answered, I almost whooped. "Hey, it's me."

"Hello, love. What can I do you for?"

"Can you spare thirty minutes? I need to go somewhere, and it's kind of urgent." My leg bounced up and down under the table. *Please say yes. Please say yes.*

"Hang on a sec." She must have covered the phone because I could hear muffled rustling. "Okay. Are you at your place?"

"Yes."

"I'll be there in ten minutes. Hold tight."

"Thank you so, so much! Bye." I looked at Lavender. "One of Will's colleagues is on her way. Can I ask you a favour?"

"Mmm, ask away. I don't guarantee I'll grant that favour, but you can always ask." His lips curled up cheekily at the corners.

"Can you lend me ten thousand pounds?"

His eyes widened. "What?! I hardly know you. The answer would be no."

I pouted and made a sad face. "Oh, that's too bad. Well, if you won't do that, maybe you'd be kind enough to record the conversation you have with Luisa's parents so Will can listen to it later?"

He waggled a finger at me. "Oh, you're good. Comparing the favour you want to a ridiculous one so it seems small in comparison. The thing is, won't I be invading their privacy? Isn't something like that illegal?"

"I have no idea, but once we find Sarah, we'll delete it. We might have to listen to it a couple of times to make sure we get all the information out if it we need. We can't afford to miss anything. Please?"

Lavender huffed. "I don't like it… but okay." He rolled his eyes. "How do I get myself into these things?" He shook his head.

I smiled sweetly and batted my lashes. "You just can't resist my awesomeness."

He grinned. "Yep, that must be it."

After a few minutes, a knock sounded on the reception-room door. I jumped up. "That's her!" I hadn't hung out with Imani for ages, so I was excited. Sad, really, considering this was kind of an investigation and Sarah was missing, but it was more about having the support. Friends made things bearable when you thought there was no way you'd get through.

I opened the door. "Hello!"

She stepped forward and hugged me. "Hello, lovie. What's the emergency?"

"Has Will said anything to you?"

She pressed her lips together and furrowed her brow. "No. What happened?"

"Sarah's been missing since this morning, but because we really have no proof of foul play, and it's only been a few hours, it's not like we can open a real investigation. We're doing a little one on the side. We think it has something to do with that heist at the fashion show the other night."

"Where's Will?"

"Ma'am has him tied up with something. He was with me this morning, and we visited Luisa's place in Florence." I brought her up to speed on where we were at with the statements and why we needed to go and see Luisa's parents.

"Okay. Cool. I'm on board."

A fraction of the tension that had solidified my neck and shoulder muscles lessened. "Thank you so much. Come through, and I'll introduce you to Sarah's friend Lavender. After that, we can go."

"Lead the way."

When we entered, Lavender stood and held out his hand. "Lavender Lau at your service."

Imani smiled and grabbed his hand. "Lovely to meet you." She regarded him for a moment. "Ah, so you're a witch too. That makes life easier."

Lavender nodded. "It does, rather. Luisa doesn't know, so if we happen to run into her, we need to be hush-hush."

"Okay," Imani said. "Hopefully we can find Sarah this afternoon. I'm sure Will is going out of his mind, albeit quietly."

"Yeah, pretty much." I looked at Lavender. "So, you know where her parents live. I'll leave this going-there bit up to you. How are we doing this?"

"The usual way, unless you want to ride my magic carpet." He laughed.

I narrowed my eyes, not sure if he was joking. "Do those things exist?"

Imani looked at me as if I'd just lost twenty IQ points. "You're serious?"

I shrugged. "Well, witches exist. Why not flying carpets? You could spell a Persian rug to fly if you felt like it."

Imani didn't look convinced. "Hmm, I suppose you could. It would take a lot of power though. You wouldn't get very far. Travelling is way more efficient." She looked at Lavender. "Okay, smarty-pants, we're travelling, but where are we going, and how are we playing this when we get there?"

Lavender threw his head back, like a testy prancing horse. "Lily and I have discussed this, and it's better if I interview by myself but record it so you and Will can listen later. This isn't an official investigation, so I've been told. It's best if we keep you out of it." He looked at me. "Is that about right, Lily?"

"Yep."

Lavender twirled his earring. "They live in Florence as well, about fifteen minutes' drive from Luisa, closer to the centre of town."

"Hang on a sec." Imani pulled her phone out of her pocket and searched Google Maps. "What's the street name?"

"Piazza Massimo D'Azeglio."

Her tongue poked out slightly between her closed lips as she typed in the address. After a moment, she said, "Excellent. We have a PIB landing spot about three blocks from there." She stared at Lavender. "This one is private—you can't tell anyone about it. We don't want witches using our resources and jamming the system. We also don't want it to look suspicious—too many people leaving the toilets without having gone in first is going to grab attention pretty quickly."

This witching thing didn't get less confusing, which was totally irritating. "But don't witches use quite a few different public toilets?"

"Yes, but some of the ones we've used have been PIB exclusive—not all, mind you. Some of the PIB ones are in buildings that could pose a security risk if the general witch public were to know the coordinates. Anything that can be locked up at a certain time or somewhere that contains important artefacts or people, even places someone could break into if they had bathroom access. This is one such building." She turned back to Lavender. "Will you promise on a spell?"

"Yes." Gee, he must really trust us now—there was no argument as there had been when Will had asked the same question. "Hit me." He stood still, waiting.

Imani's magic vibrated the hair on the back of my neck. "Say exactly what I say: I promise never to repeat the following information to anyone. If I do, I consent to the loss of my right pinkie finger." My mouth dropped open. Witches really had a dislike of pinkie fingers. That's similar to what Will had promised. It was odd that I didn't see pinkie fingers just lying in the streets—surely all witches weren't that good at keeping promises or secrets. And what happened after you lost your pinkie? Next time, did you have to swear using the ring finger? I was going to check out witches' hands from now on—the ones with missing digits likely couldn't be trusted.

Lavender repeated after Imani, and a little bell tinkled. Hmm, did it tinkle again if you broke your promise, or was it more of a deep ba-bow sound like the one on *Family Feud* when a contestant got the answer wrong? That would be rather dramatic to have that sound as your finger fell off. And it might happen in front of other people. How embarrassing. Everyone would know you couldn't be trusted. And did the finger cauterize instantly, or did it spurt out blood?

Oh my God! Is that where the tradition of pinkie promises came from? Naughty Japanese, trying to take all the credit with their *yubikiri*.

"Lily?" Imani was waving her hand in front of my face.

"Oh, sorry. Just… well, you know." I gave her a hopeless smile.

"Yes, love, I know." She shook her head and laughed. "Okay, we're ready to go. Since you weren't paying attention, Lily, you can come through my door. Just be careful."

"Thanks." She made her doorway, and I stepped through, careful to keep my whole body inside the frame, including my pinkies—I might need them later, plus I didn't want other witches to look at me as if I couldn't be trusted.

I hurried out of the stall to make room for Imani. As I stepped out, I checked my no-notice spell. Phew. I hadn't undone it since last time. I carefully snuck past a woman washing her hands and through the door. Just down the hall, Lavender was exiting another door. Imani stopped behind me just as he reached us. By the clinical smell and hushed atmosphere, it was clear we were in a hospital. The interior was clean and modern, with fawn-coloured tiled floors. We hurried past the timber-panelled reception desk, which was unmanned, and through the glass front entry.

Outside, the building looked rather old, maybe four hundred years or so. I had not seen that coming. The tall archways and ornate stone detailing made me want to grab my camera and take some photos. *Stop, Lily*! I chastised myself.

Seriously, I had to learn to focus. As I was gawking, Lavender and Imani had hurried off. I jogged to catch up.

During our three-block walk, I did my best to take everything in while making sure I stayed with them. Before long, we arrived at Piazza Massimo D'Azeglio, which appeared to be a large park. Lavender stopped. "Wait here. I'm going to that building over there." He pointed to a five-storey building across the road.

He turned, and I said, "Don't forget to record everything." He held his hand above his head and waved as he walked off. Imani and I waited on a park bench. Even though it was chilly, a couple of mothers with their children strolled past to the playground area. I made a bubble of silence. "Are you going to the meeting tonight?"

"Yes, of course. We really need to figure out what to do next. It's only a matter of time before bloody RP try something else. It's been too long since we worked on it."

I blew a few strands of hair from my face. "Tell me about it. I'm sick of living with this too." I pointed to my arm, where my sleeve covered the tattoo. "Who knows what it might do to me next."

Sympathy shone from her eyes. "I heard what happened. Scary stuff. Did it leave a mark?"

"Nope. But it hurt like hell at the time." I looked around, paranoia giving me an adrenaline shot.

"Hey, don't worry. They can't follow you now that the tracking on that thing's been disabled."

"Yeah, I know, but I still worry." There wasn't much else to say, so we sat in tense silence until Lavender returned twenty minutes later.

I stood. "Tell me everything."

"It was a fruitful expedition. But I think this is better

discussed somewhere private, maybe back at your place?" I looked at Imani, and she nodded.

"Okay. Let's go." As we made our way back to the hospital toilets, I texted Will, just in case he could meet us at home, but he didn't respond. What the hell did Angelica have him doing? Surely he'd mentioned Sarah was missing? My stomach bubbled like a cauldron full of demons. Okay, so I'd never seen a cauldron full of demons, but I imagined it writhed and gave one an eerie sensation in the pit of their stomach and probably smelled bad—not that I smelled....

We all made our own doorways to return to Angelica's. I arrived first and unlocked the reception-room door. When Imani and Lavender came through to the hallway, I locked the door, and we convened at the kitchen table. I magicked myself a cappuccino—I was in desperate need of a pick-me-up. "Spill, Lav. What did her parents say?"

"Well, if you're having a drink, so can I." A margarita with a little green umbrella appeared on the table. He picked it up and sipped, then placed it back on the table. "Her parents were not the recipients of any of those gifts. They also told me that she was looking to move back in with them and rent her apartment out—money problems, apparently."

Yikes. "Well, there's our motivation for stealing the money."

Lavender slid down in his seat and drained the rest of his glass, then squinted his eyes shut and gripped his head with one hand. "Gah, brain freeze."

Imani looked at me, one eyebrow raised. I should really explain things to her—Lavender wasn't as ditzy as he appeared. "Luisa was a good friend of his and Sarah's. He's struggling to believe she would have money problems because she wasn't exactly tight, but she was careful with her money, and she was earning a lot as a model. I think he's having a crisis about not knowing his friend very well."

He sat up straighter. "That's not it at all, sweetie. Something bad is going on. I just know it. Her parents were worried, and not because of the jewellery heist. They said she's been acting weird since about November—she's been vague, not wanting to spend time with them, evasive about letting them know where she's been. They're sure she's on drugs."

"What do you think?" Imani asked.

He shook his head. "Not drugs. She'd never touch the stuff."

I cocked my head to the side. "But you and Sarah both swore she wouldn't steal anything, and look what happened. You also thought she was careful with her money, but it turns out, she's a shopaholic." I huffed out a loud breath. "Whatever she's doing, where does Sarah fit into all this? Did she just stumble upon her and has paid the price?"

His eyes widened as far as they'd go. "No. Never." I opened my mouth to argue, but he held up his hand and tutted. "Before you say something else I can't stand to hear, believe me when I say that she would never hurt her friends. This whole thing reeks of blackmail, or something else."

Imani tapped her pointer finger on the table. "Or coercion, maybe?"

"Possibly." He magicked another margarita into his hand.

Imani raised a brow. "Please don't get drunk. We have enough to deal with." She waved her hand, and it disappeared.

He sucked in a breath. "You didn't!"

Imani's tone was deadly serious. "I did. Someone needs to take control here. You're both way out of your depths."

A noise came from the hallway. I swivelled my head

around to watch the door. Will walked through, his grey eyes barely containing the tempest within. I wasn't sure whether to give him a hug or some space. Instead of rushing to him, I stayed where I was. "Are you okay?"

He growled one word. "Chad."

"Ah," Imani and I said simultaneously. That explained everything.

Imani pulled out the chair next to her. "Sit. We have news and a recording Lavender took of his interview with Luisa's parents."

Will sat, leaving his chair pulled out, and stretched his long legs out in front. Lavender placed his phone on the table and pressed play on the recording. We listened to the twenty-minute conversation, which Lavender had summed up to us before. When it was done, Will folded his arms and stared at the wall. We waited for him to say something.

"Right. So we have motive for her to steal the jewellery. But where is my sister?" He sat up straight and eyeballed Lavender. "Let's assume my sister went to see Luisa but didn't find her at her apartment." Okay, so we knew she had been there from my photos, but Lavender didn't. "Where would she go next? Her parents said neither she nor Sarah had visited them since the incident. Do you think they were telling the truth?"

Crap! I should've taken photos outside their building to confirm whether or not Sarah had been there. I looked at Will. "Um, we could go back to… check."

"What, like see if there are security cameras anywhere that might have caught her?" Lavender said.

"Yes, that exactly," said Will. "Failing that, where else would Luisa go? Does she have any other close friends?"

Lavender shrugged. "A couple of school friends, and a couple of models."

"Didn't they check out those models after everything happened?" I asked.

Will gave me a nod. "Yes."

"So," Imani said, "we visit the friends." She looked at Lavender. "Do you have their addresses?"

"No, but we could probably get them from her parents since we're going back there anyway."

Will stood and looked down at the make-up artist. "Same as before, you can interview the friends, and we'll wait outside. We don't want to spook them, and if work finds out I was using my authority as a government agent to question people when there's no investigation, I could lose my job."

Imani stood and looked at Will. "Here are the coordinates. You take Lily, and I'll take Lavender."

Will waited until Imani and Lavender left before he said, "Take photos this time."

"Okay. I'm so sorry that I didn't think of it last time. I'm so stupid."

He gave me a hug. "You are not stupid. You're not an agent. I don't expect you to think of everything—even though you're amazing, you're not perfect. No one is. Thank you for helping me out with this." He kissed the top of my head, and I squeezed him hard.

"It's my pleasure. I love you, and I'd do anything to fix what's wrong. I care about Sarah too, you know. She's a pretty awesome woman."

He released me and looked away. He made his doorway and gestured for me to use it. "You first, madam." I stepped through and crossed my fingers we'd find her soon. Unfortunately, I didn't think we would.

CHAPTER 6

Bar Fondi was an adorable little bar and café establishment in Rome. That's right, Rome. After Lavender questioned Luisa's friends and I took photos on the streets outside their buildings—discovering that Sarah had visited both of them—we decided to hold a meeting and eat before we took our next step. And, no, we hadn't told Lavender about the photos.

I sipped my coffee and nibbled my ham and cheese panini while, under the protection of a bubble of silence, Lavender told us everything he'd found out. According to the time Luisa's friend Anita had seen them, it meant Sarah hadn't been missing for quite as long as we thought, but only by an hour. We were taking that as positive news.

"After Anita told Sarah that she hadn't seen Luisa for a month, she did tell her that Luisa had texted her two weeks ago and told her she was meeting her ex for lunch. Other than that, she didn't give Sarah anything much."

"So, we check the ex's house?" That seemed the logical

conclusion. Not that she'd definitely be there, but it was all we had.

Imani finished her cappuccino. "That's all we have to go on, so yes. I'm thinking you have his address, Lavender?"

"Yep. I sure do. He was renting, though, so we'd better hope he hasn't moved."

Will downed his espresso in one gulp and ran a hand through his hair. He looked at me with tired eyes. "I hope we're not chasing around like this tomorrow. We're running out of places to look."

I grabbed his hand and squeezed. "We'll find her. I assume you've tried tracking her phone?"

He nodded. "It's off."

I sighed. Of course it was. As if he wouldn't have tried that in the first place. "Well, let's get Lavender to question the ex. He's a witch, so we need to tread carefully."

Imani looked at Lavender. "Do you know how to create a mind shield? We don't want him reading your mind without you realising—it could be his special skill."

"Ah, yes, but I haven't done it for a long time. Hang on and let me put it up, then try and read my mind." His magic came across as playful as it cascaded down my scalp. "I'm ready."

Imani and Will both stared at Lavender, concentration on their faces. After a minute, they sat back. Will gave a hint of a smile. "You've got a strong shield. Nice work."

Lavender smiled and puffed out his chest. "Thank you." His face grew serious. "How do you want me to play this?"

Will rubbed his chin. "He'll think it's weird if you ask about Sarah. Maybe say you're worried about Luisa, and you haven't heard from her, and that her family asked you to see if you could find her. Also say that in light of the theft, you want Luisa to know you're her friend and you just want to know she's okay. Say that you know she cared about him and you figured she may have reached out to him; that's why you're there."

"Should I record it on my phone again?"

Will and Imani shared a quick look. I couldn't tell what they were trying to communicate, but after their second-long private conference, Will magicked something to his hand, something small. "Here. Wear this. It will transmit your conversation, even if someone casts a bubble of silence. It's the latest tech that only a highly trained operative would be able to find. It emits such a low level of magic that it's hidden from any normal person trying to detect a spying device with their own spell. Criminals evolve, and so must we." He handed it over.

Lavender held the tiny black ball in his hand. It kind of looked like a dead fly. "Where should I put it?"

"It's highly sensitive. If you place it on your shoulder, just under your jumper, that will do—it's magicked to stick. Just don't move too much when someone's talking, or it will pick up the interference instead."

"Okay." He slipped his hand under the collar of his jumper. "This is kind of fun, being a spy for a day."

"Just be careful," said Imani. "When you come across a criminal, they can be unpredictable and dangerous, and we have no idea what her ex is like. He might be a great guy and have nothing that could help us. He could, however, be just the person we're looking for. We'll be out of sight but close by. If anything happens, we'll be there in an instant."

"Thanks." Lavender stood. "Are we ready?"

I swallowed the last of my panini and stood. "Yep."

Imani and Will got up, and we headed for Roma Termini—the train station, which was just around the block. We had to pay one euro each to use the toilets because there were automatic gates leading to them, and if we'd magicked them open, we'd have been breaking the law. I didn't see how sneaking out was any different, but we weren't actually using them to do anything someone would have to clean, and we weren't using their toilet paper, so it was irritating to have to pay. I wasn't against breaking the law when said law made no sense.

Imani and I squished unnoticed into one cubicle. It was pretty small, as, I supposed, most were. She'd gone in first and turned to face me. There was barely two inches between us. "Turn around," she whispered. I did as asked. "Now back up until your back is against my front." I scooted closer until I couldn't go any further. "Okay, now hold still. I'm going to make my doorway around us."

There was a brief moment of vertigo before a familiar bathroom appeared around us—the train station at Florence. I hadn't travelled so much in my whole life as I had today. At least witches could cover a lot of ground quickly. I hated to think what a non-witch would do if they couldn't find a loved one. Getting places the normal way wasted so much time.

We met up with Will and Lavender on the concourse, then hurried outside. This was my version of *Groundhog Day* but without the benefit of a do-over tomorrow to fix what we got wrong. Just as we reached a taxi, Will's phone rang. He snatched it out of his pocket. "Hello." His firm tone would have scared even the hardiest of nuisance callers. He put up his hand for us to stop. His forehead wrinkled, and his lips pinched together. "You're sure? …yes. Hang on." His magic tingled my scalp as he reached into his pocket and pulled out a notepad and pen. He handed them to me. "Write down the address I'm about to give you." I nodded as he listened to whoever was on the phone. He gave me the information, and I recorded it. "Okay, thanks. Um, I'm just at the basilica. I'll be there as soon as I can. Bye." Huh? What basilica? I thought this was a train station.

Lavender was about to get into a taxi, but Imani shook her head. "Not now." She turned to Will. "Where to?" She was in work mode—she'd anticipated what Will needed and was making sure it happened quickly.

He took a deep breath. "Someone's found Sarah. She's alive but confused. They didn't tell me much, said it was better if we came and got her. Mine was the only number she could remember."

My heartbeat raced with the shot of adrenaline. She'd better be okay. Alive was a good start, but there were different degrees of being alive. "Where is she?"

"Mallorca." Before I could ask where it was, Will clarified. "A Spanish island." I blinked. What the hell? I wanted to ask how she got there, and a million other things, but he knew as much as I did, or was that as little....

Imani planted her hands on her hips. "Right, so you said basilica, as in Catedral-Basilica de Santa Maria de Palma?"

"Yes."

How did she know? Were they talking to each other via thoughts? And why would he say that? "Um, why did you tell them you were there?"

"So they don't think it's strange when we turn up in Spain within half an hour from being Florence, which would be impossible, even if you had a helicopter, and the average Joe doesn't have a helicopter at their disposal. Come on. Back to the toilets." What a romantic offer. I stifled a smile. Well, it wasn't every day the man you loved gave such an order. "Imani has the coordinates—it's one of those special PIB landing places I was talking about before. And make sure you keep your no-notices on until we get out of the church. We need to drop them so it's not confusing for the people who have Sarah. Let's go." He turned and jogged back inside, the rest of us following. He made a good point. I wondered what would happen if you talked to people with your no-notice spell activated. Would it be like talking to a man who seemed to be listening, but then when you finished speaking, he had no clue what you just said?

Imani's doorway came out in a dark place. The floor was hard, and a faint earthy odour tickled my nostrils. I held my hands out in front to feel for a wall as I carefully stepped forward—if Will and Lavender came in now, they'd end up walking into us, and who knew what disaster would unfold. Light burst into the darkness, and I blinked. Imani stood there with her phone torch on. Why was I so stupid? I should have thought of that.

And there was the door, set in a stone wall. Imani reached it first. I stayed close to her, trying to make sure I was out of the way for Will. He soon exited his doorway after Lavender.

Will kept his voice low, not that anyone would hear us in this solid room. "Just pretend we're sightseers who got lost if we're noticed by anyone. When we leave this room, we'll go up a flight of stairs, into a corridor, and then into the main cathedral." Were we underground? My eyes widened. What if we were in a crypt with icky dead bodies. Ew. I swallowed my fear, but sweat still popped out on my face. I reached for the door, wanting out as soon as possible. "Yes, you can open it, Lily. Good on you for asking." In my state of discomfort, his sarcasm was dead to me. Ick, there was that word again. Had someone been buried in the room we were in? Did something just touch my neck? I shuddered and wrenched the door open. A gush of cold air surged over me as I jumped into a hallway.

While I tried to catch my breath, Will and Imani smirked at my freak-out. "What's got you all bothered, love?" Amusement frolicked in her tone.

"It's creepy. That's all."

"You're the one who doesn't believe in ghosts." She had a point, but my brain didn't care. The logic train had left without me today.

I jogged down the hallway. "Lily, where are you going?" Will called out.

I stopped and turned. "Anywhere that isn't here?"

He chuckled and shook his head. "We need to go this way."

"Oh." I quickly joined them. Will led the way to a staircase and up. We came out in a small corridor, and then the church opened in front of us. Wow.... Soaring ceilings, gothic architecture, stained-glass windows—it had everything on a grand scale. But we didn't have time to linger, and I only managed to check it out as we fast walked towards the exit. It was probably rude to run in a church, even though none of the many sightseers ambling through the building would notice.

Outside, the familiar tang of salty air made it feel like home. I hadn't had much time to miss Sydney, but the moment invited melancholy. I missed my modest but comfy unit near the beach, and my friends. Would I ever go back? I shook my head. Now wasn't the time to ponder the future.

The late-afternoon sun shone weakly, but the vibrancy of the blue ocean and the huge water feature in front of the cathedral wasn't diminished. It was a few degrees warmer than Florence but still chilly. Palm trees lined the waterfront in the distance, and yachts dotted the sea. The church was on a high point surrounded by pedestrian pathways. Before we set off, I dropped my no-notice spell. Yay me for remembering!

It took a minute to reach the road. Once there, it took more time to find a taxi. Will finally nabbed one, and we jumped in. My leg bounced up and down on the drive. Even though Will had told the driver where we were going, I had no idea where that was and how long it would take, and no one spoke. I didn't want to ask anything in case Will needed this time to think through what was going on, so I just stared at the passing scenery on the coastal road, which comprised light-coloured buildings, trees, countless yacht masts—I didn't think I'd ever seen so many marinas—and the ocean.

Our trip ended some twenty-five minutes later at an immaculate four-storey white structure that looked out over the water. Nice, if you liked upmarket apartment complexes on the beach—and who didn't?

Will asked the driver to wait, although there were going to be five of us on the return trip, so we wouldn't all fit. Maybe one of us would have to travel from somewhere nearby to get home?

"Do you know this place?" I asked Lavender. If Sarah had come here looking for Luisa, it stood to reason that Lavender also knew about the place.

He looked around. "No. I've never been here before, and trust me, I'd remember. Look at that view." As we walked up the path, past a humungous blue-tiled infinity pool, to the security entry, he walked backwards and gazed at the ocean.

Will buzzed the intercom for the concierge. A young dark-haired woman in a white shirt and blue pencil skirt answered the door. "Are you William?" Her Spanish accent made her way too sexy for my liking. *Get a grip, Lily. She can't help it.* I really needed to get on top of my self-esteem issues.

"Yes. You have my sister here?"

"Yes. Please come in. She's in the manager's office." As we crossed the shiny white-tiled floor, she filled us in, the clack of her black high heels as loud as her voice. "One of our residents is a doctor, and we've had him examine her. He thinks she should go to hospital for more tests, but she refused. She insisted we call you." We reached a door, and she opened it. "Please, after you."

We all filed into the small office. With only a desk, office chair, one guest chair, and a plant in a corner behind the desk, it was rather cramped. Sarah was sitting in the chair behind the desk, hunched over, her head resting on her arms on the desk. She briefly looked up—just enough to acknowledge us —then dropped her head back down. Thank God she was alive, but she did not look okay. I hurried over and rubbed her back.

An olive-skinned, balding man, who'd been sitting in the chair opposite Sarah, stood and turned to shake Will's hand. The man's demeanour was calm and authoritative. "I'm Doctor Garcia. You are Sarah's brother?"

"Yes. I'm William. Pleased to meet you. Gracias for taking care of Sarah." Will quickly extricated himself from the greeting and, in two large strides, made it to Sarah's chair. He gently lifted her head and scrutinised her face. "Are you well enough to travel?" I'm sure he didn't want to have any conversations here. Her response was a tiny nod and squint before she shut her eyes.

Imani introduced herself to Dr Garcia. "What's your prognosis?"

"I'd like her to have more tests. She has marks on her wrists and grazes on her palms. There is no sign of other trauma, which makes her memory loss more… worrying. She might have been drugged, but we can't know unless we test her blood."

Imani nodded, then turned to the woman I assumed was the manager. "Where did you find her?"

"By the pool. I didn't recognise her, so I wanted to say hello and find out if she was staying here, maybe as a guest of someone. When I approached her, she ignored me, which I thought odd. When I spoke loudly and she still didn't respond, I realised there was something wrong."

"Can you show me exactly where? I'd like to take some photos, in case the police need to be called in." So, Imani wasn't divulging she was from a British government agency. That probably made sense because they wouldn't have had jurisdiction here… at least I didn't think so. I knew the PIB had branches around the world, but who knew if they had to stick to their own areas? Imani looked at me. "Come with me, Lily. Will and Lavender can take Sarah back to our hotel, and we'll call our own doctor for testing. I'd rather have her comfortable."

"That sounds like a great idea," said Will as he draped Sarah's arm around his neck and scooped her out of the chair. She gave a wan smile and closed her eyes. I gave Will a concerned look. She needed help. What had they done to her? Had it been Luisa? So many questions, as usual.

We waited for Will and Lavender to exit before following the manager to the pool area. I knew what I was there for, so I took out my phone. It would be good to get real-time photos of the crime scene and photos to show who had brought her here. We were gathering evidence—both magical and physical.

The manager showed us which pool lounge she'd been lying on. I got to work photographing the scene. As Imani checked things out, she asked, "Have you questioned anyone in the complex to see whether anyone saw how she got here?"

"No. I would think the police should do that, but I wanted to wait for Sarah's brother to arrive. We can't know if it was an assault or if she just drank too much or took drugs. She says she doesn't remember how she arrived here, but the police may not take this seriously."

"Do you have security cameras?"

"Only in the lobby and underground car park." A crackling voice speaking in Spanish came from her hand. She was carrying a walkie-talkie, which I hadn't noticed before. "Excuse me," she said to Imani before answering it in Spanish. After a brief conversation, she addressed us. "I'm sorry, but something else requires my attention." She reached into her shirt pocket. "If you need access to the security videos, I can only provide them with a court order or request from the police. But this is my card." She handed it to Imani. "Do you have a card? If I hear anything from the residents, I can let you know."

Imani reached into her pocket and pulled out her card. Did it say PIB? I doubted it but wondered what it said. "Here. You can get me on that number or email. I might check in with you tomorrow, just in case."

"Okay. Take all the time you need." She gave a nod and walked back towards the building.

Imani's magic feathered my scalp. "There's a magic signature!"

I changed from taking normal photos to using my talent. "Show me the moment Sarah arrived." She was just there, alone. "I can't see that anyone brought her here. And she's lying down in the picture, so she didn't walk." I stared at

Imani. "Is it possible someone translocated her? That would take a ridiculous amount of energy, wouldn't it?"

"Yes." She looked up and turned in a full circle, surveying everything. "They couldn't have translocated her very far. Maybe from a car on the street or from one of the apartments. I would say they couldn't have been more than seventy-five metres away."

"Is it possible that the signature is from another witch doing something harmless, like pruning the hedges?" The grounds were well groomed, which indicated a regular gardener. Ah, lifestyles of the rich and famous.

"It could be. We'll have to question more people. Firstly, we'll need to find out if Sarah was drugged. At least we can put the PIB onto it then. We might have to liaise with the Spanish office, get their permission to work in their jurisdiction, but considering the crime this relates to was committed in London, it shouldn't be too difficult. Once we've established Sarah didn't turn up here on her own, we can question the residents and anyone who might have been working this morning. We'll also grab those security tapes."

"Could this have been done by a non-witch?"

She pursed her lips. "I don't think so. There would be no way of getting her here so quickly from the UK or France or even Florence. Unless a non-witch lured her here, knowing she could travel. But I can't imagine she's told any non-witches about what she is. We'll have to wait and see."

Imani made some notes on a small pad of paper she pulled from her pocket. Once she was done, she looked up. "Ready to go?"

"Yep. Lead the way."

We donned our no-notice spells, found the nearest public toilet, and travelled back to Angelica's. Relief at having found

Sarah stopped the sick feeling in the pit of my stomach, but we still had to solve the riddle of how and why she disappeared, oh, and we had a meeting tonight about RP.

The fun just never stopped.

Ever.

CHAPTER 7

I sat at my brother's dining-room table with Imani, Will, James, Millicent, Beren, and Liv. Ma'am sat at the head of the table and folded her hands in front of her on the tabletop. I yawned. What a mammoth day. Once Will got Sarah back to Angelica's, he'd called Beren in to heal her, but there was a major problem: she'd lost her memory of today, yesterday, and, in fact, the last three weeks. And by lost, I meant a witch had tampered with her memory. Beren said it was lucky she hadn't lost more—wiping part of someone's memory was a dangerous business, and usually didn't end well. The only positive was that we had a magic signature, and Angelica had started a case file. The PIB were involved now, which was a good thing.

Because of her traumatic day, Sarah was in no shape to go to the hotel or turn up for work. Lavender had to go back to work, but we got Will's mum to come and stay at Angelica's until we returned home. Right now, it was time to plot our next move in the search for my parents. Guilt kneed me in the stomach—I hadn't thought of them as much in the last week as I should've. *I'm sorry, Mum, Dad. I haven't forgotten you.* I blinked back pesky moisture.

Angelica clapped once, loudly. I started, jerking back, and my chair almost tipped over. Will grabbed it just in time. Hand on heart, I thanked him and tried to get my breathing under control. Way to try and kill me. Jeez.

"Is everyone ready?" she asked, pointedly looking at me. I rolled my eyes but said nothing. She'd get annoyed enough by my eye-rolling, but it wasn't likely to push her over the edge and get me into more trouble. It was my little way of telling her what she could do with her accusing stare when she'd been the one to scare me. I had been ready. Even though I'd been thinking about something else, I would have come back to earth when she'd started talking.

Call me crazy, but was that the tiniest of smiles on her face? Hmm, no; her poker face was reengaged. Maybe she'd had gas? "Good evening, all. It's been a busy day." She waited for our sighs of agreement to finish before she continued. "I just want to start by apologising on behalf of Millicent's dad, Robert. He's unable to make it tonight, but"—she looked at me—"he's keen to tee up a day and time for you to get together and work on that tattoo."

I nodded. "Thanks." I looked at Millicent. "Tell him there's no hurry. I know this thing isn't easy." I held up the offending arm, then let it drop back into my lap. Robert had successfully disabled the tracking on my tattoo, which was better than nothing. I was upset about the potential for more pain attacks from RP, but trying to disable the snake embedded in my skin was risky in itself. It was almost a lose-lose proposition at this point. I ignored the swarm of fear that rushed my belly.

"Since we're all here, I'd like to give an update on Sarah's blood work. We found Rohypnol." I sucked in a breath. It wasn't a total surprise, considering how out of it she'd been when we picked her up, but I'd expected magic had caused her problems. Oh my God, had she been raped? Will gripped my hand and kept his eyes on Ma'am, waiting for the rest. Ma'am met his gaze. "We've had our new doctor from the PIB examine her, and other than the scrapes on her palms and rope burn on her wrists, there was no other sign of trauma… inside or out."

Will dropped his head back and stared at the ceiling for a moment, likely trying to compose himself. Relief gusted through the room, like a cool change on a hot day.

Ma'am flashed a rare smile. "I'm just glad it's not worse. We'll have a meeting about it tomorrow at headquarters. I'd like everyone there at eight in the morning, please. Right, now that's done, we can move onto why we're here." She looked my way. "I'm sorry we've been neglecting this, Lily. I've unearthed some information that bears further investigation." Oh, wow, okay. I bit my bottom lip and bounced my leg under the table. "The video you took at the Birmingham Conference Centre with all the politicians has yielded fruit." She turned to the wall behind her. Her magic pattered on my scalp, and a large TV screen appeared. The photo I'd taken of Dana's father and the politician with the slicked-back hair was large and clear. "This man, Graham Clarke MP"—she pointed to the stranger—"also has links with a mutual acquaintance of theirs." She flicked her hand, and another image appeared. "This is a still from the video you captured. His name is Vlad Kovalevsky." He'd been sitting on the table with my mother. Seeing her was unexpected, and I had to bite my tongue so I wouldn't cry. Damned sorrow.

Vlad was tall, wide-shouldered, had thinning fair hair, although the lighting wasn't that great, so it was hard to tell exactly what colour it was—maybe it was blond, maybe it was red, or light brown. He was maybe mid-forties. His strong jaw was bluntly square, almost like a cartoon superhero, and his eyes were too close together for my liking.

Papers appeared on the table—a few in front of each person. "We have some intel on them—not enough, I'll admit—but it's enough to make a start. Please read that now; then we'll chat."

I picked mine up. After reading through everything, I had a basic picture of the trio's relationship. Vlad supplied cheap Eastern European labour for Dana's father's manufacturing plant in Manchester, and the politician was someone Dana's father spoke to regularly, according to the politician's email records. Was that even allowed? The PIB had hacked into this guy's emails. That had to be illegal. I looked up. "Ma'am?"

"Yes, dear."

"You've risked a lot to get this info, haven't you."

"We do what we must." I waited a moment in case she had anything else to say, but, nope, that was it.

"Was there anything important in those emails?"

"Unfortunately, not much. Maybe this was an account he didn't mind being hacked. It could be a cover so that anyone prying would assume that's it and move on. We have enough to link them as having a consistent relationship. What Graham Clarke does for Dana's father is anyone's guess. It could range from turning a blind eye to workplace breaches, helping him get lucrative government contracts, or even helping him obtain manufacturing approvals for industrial uses that wouldn't normally be allowed. This is what we need to find out, amongst other things." I put up my hand. "Yes, dear?"

"I'm not sure what this has to do with my parents' disappearance? Maybe this is just a side thing that isn't important."

Ma'am looked at me, worry and confusion on her face. Her words were spoken slowly, as if I was a simpleton or maybe someone who couldn't speak English. "Lily, why do you think your mother was there?"

My cheeks heated. Oh, that's what she was getting at. "You think she was close to figuring out something that threatened this business arrangement?"

"Thank you for saving me from having to explain it to the nth degree. Please think before you speak next time. And, yes, I think she must have been close to a discovery when she disappeared, but…" She pressed her lips closed.

I cocked my head to the side. "But what?"

Poker face reassembled, she shook her head. "But nothing. Just me thinking out loud." I narrowed my eyes. What had she been about to say, and why decide not to tell us? Was she hiding something? She turned to James. "I have Chad and the directors breathing down my neck at the moment. I'd like you to work out a plan of attack and deal with it because I don't have time. And don't bother me with the details, please. I trust your judgement." What? I stuck my finger in my ear to see if it was blocked. Surely I didn't hear what I thought I'd heard.

James blinked and opened his mouth to speak, but the words stalled—this was obviously unexpected for him, too, and he was doing his best not to question it. He eventually managed, "Yes, Ma'am."

She gave him a small smile. "Thank you. In light of the PIB investigating Sarah's brief disappearance, I have a lot of work to do, so I'm going to leave. As I've said, please don't brief me on anything to do with your next steps. I trust you'll all do a wonderful job. I'll give the floor to James, and I expect you'll show him the same respect you show me." She magicked some papers into her hand and gave them to James before standing. "Everything you need to commence with the next phase of this investigation is there. If you have any questions, let me know." She gave him the subtlest of head shakes. Was she telling him again not to keep her updated? She made her doorway. "Goodnight, all. I'll see you bright and early tomorrow morning." Without any fanfare, she was gone.

I stared at my brother across the table. "What the hell just happened?"

He shrugged. "I'm not sure." He sounded distracted, likely because he was wracking his brain for an answer. I betted he had suspicions but wouldn't share them—what was she hiding? Whatever the secret, I was guessing it wasn't that she had a two-week spa visit booked in.

James stared at the table for a moment, then looked at each of us in turn. "We have work to do, team. Ma'am's left it in our capable hands, so let's discuss what's next." He scanned the papers she'd given him. "Right. Ma'am's looked into what she could—financials of the three men, property ownership, that kind of thing. She couldn't find any transactions between them, but she's made a note that it's only what she could find. They likely have offshore bank accounts in tax havens under company names we can't identify. Because there are witches involved, this is going to be much harder than if it were a non-witch trying to hide financial transactions. Our easiest target is the politician since he's not a witch." His gaze met mine. "Lily, you're going to have to gather evidence for us with your camera. We're also going to have to check out that factory. Whatever they're trying to fly under the radar for could be the very thing that will lead us to Vlad and Dana's father. I'd like to get Imani and Millicent on the case. We can't be obvious, and as much as I hate to say it, women snooping around somewhere are less suspicious than men. We'll need to come up with some kind of cover for you to be around the factory, and you ladies don't have the time to be undercover. Any suggestions?"

I hoped someone else had something because I had nothin'. Thank God Imani piped up. "What does the factory make?"

James answered, "Pharmaceuticals. They're contracted to produce them for other companies."

Imani rested her hands on the table. "So security is going to be an issue. They'll have cameras trained on every inch of the facility and probably a couple of security personnel at least. Because the owner is a witch, he probably has higher-ups who are too, which will mean a no-notice spell won't work."

Millicent pressed her lips together. "Hmm. Maybe it'll be easier to start with the politician. Can we break into his office and hack into his computer system? That would probably give us more to go on, and if we're lucky, we can avoid the factory altogether. If we do have to check that out, I can send in a rat."

"Who do you trust enough to go undercover with this?" Imani asked. "None of us have the time to weasel our way into being an employee and ingrain ourselves into the place."

Millicent laughed. "Oh, no. Sorry! I meant a real rat. We hook up a tiny camera and get it to film everything inside so we know what we're dealing with. It will take me a couple of weeks to train one, plus I'd have to find one who can understand my mind-speak enough so that it will do what we want, but it will be a hell of a lot easier than talking to a squirrel, and I managed that last month. Rats are way smarter to start with." Millicent's special talent of being able to communicate with animals had really come in handy the day of Squirrelgeddon.

I grinned. Although the memory was amusing, I didn't like that she'd slighted squirrels' intelligence. "Squirrels are smart. They're just very nervous."

Millicent smiled smugly, as if she knew everything. "Mmhmm. If you say so."

She was just teasing, but I folded my arms. "I do say so. So there." I stuck my tongue out. If she was going to treat me like a child, I might as well act like one. If you gotta do the time, may as well do the crime.

James rolled his eyes. "Come on. This is serious." And that killed the frivolities. He was right, and RP was stopping me living my life the way I wanted. Staying inside unless I was with my bodyguards—Imani or Will—rankled. The only outings I seemed to have these days was when I was working at the PIB. Oh, the fun!

Imani nodded. "I think that sounds like a good plan. We start with whatever data we can unearth, and we send the rat in to take the lay of the land. Afterwards, we can figure out how to breach the security and look around for ourselves."

Will's brow wrinkles became alarmingly deep. "I don't want Lily going there. It's too dangerous. If they're working hand in hand with RP, you're practically delivering her to them."

"Will's right." Of course James would agree with him.

"I'm not helpless, you know. What if someone went in first and created a landing spot; then I pop in, take some photos, and pop out again. We'll be doing it so the cameras don't pick us up, surely. You can tinker with them, Will. Isn't that one of your specialties?"

"Yes… when it's a place not run by witches. We can check

it out, but if the security cameras are operating with the help of magic, I may not be able to disarm them. Not to mention, there might be a magical alarm to let them know if someone's trying to disable them. They'd be on-site and looking for you within two minutes."

Bloody witches and their extra security. Okay, so I was a witch, but still.... As much as I wanted to move forward in leaps and bounds, it wasn't going to happen, and I kind of agreed with Will. Crazy, I know. "I think Will has a good point." Liv's mouth dropped open, and Will's eyes widened.

James blinked. "Well, I didn't see that coming. Are you feeling okay?"

Will put the back of his hand on my forehead. "She doesn't seem to have a fever."

Liv looked me up and down. "Maybe someone else has hijacked Lily's mind."

"Oh, for goodness' sake. If you're all going to overreact every time I agree with someone, I'll just disagree. It'll be way less dramatic."

James grinned. "You gotta admit, it's a rare thing."

"Mmm...." I wasn't going to admit to anything. "What's the plan, then?" Someone had to get this thing back on track. My stomach, which hadn't been fed for three hours, grumbled in agreement. I patted it. "I know. I know."

James looked at Will. "We'll leave the factory for now. I do like the idea of Millicent sending in a rat, though. You never know when we'll need to ditch being safe to gather more evidence." He turned to Millicent. "Can you get a rat trained up, please?"

She smiled. "Yep. I'll start looking for one tomorrow."

"Thanks." James looked at Imani. "I'd say a trip to Graham Clarke MP's office as soon as you can is in order."

"Oh, I know!" An idea had hit, and I was pretty sure it was a good one. "Why doesn't Imani write to him pretending to be someone in his electoral area. She can masquerade as a journalist wanting to interview him about the latest whatever it is he's done, and I can be her photographer. Once we're in his office, Imani can magic him to sleep, and I can take photos, see if any paperwork turns up, or anything on his laptop screen, even if he's met anyone of interest there and when. Who knows; it will possibly reveal another connection he has that's worth knowing about and help point us towards new leads."

James nodded. "That's actually a great idea."

I cocked my head to the side. "Don't act so surprised, please."

"I know I shouldn't. You constantly come to our rescue. But it's easy to underestimate someone who talks to their stomach… out loud… in a room full of people."

I gave him a confused look. "If I don't talk out loud, how is my stomach going to hear me?"

He laughed and shook his head. "I don't even know how to answer that, so I'm not going to. Let's go with my sister's suggestion. Imani, if you can tee up a meeting with him, I'll make sure you get the time away from the PIB. You won't need more than an hour. Just in case there's spying equipment in his office, I'd like you both to wear disguises. It won't do if Dana's dad realises what we're up to. Once you're in there, a small block-surveillance spell should work. I doubt they're watching him 24/7, not like they'd be watching the factory security televisions, so it's unlikely they'll see the moment the image blacks out, then changes from him at his desk to an empty room. And even if they did, they'd think it was just a glitch." From what I understood of the block-surveillance spell, it recorded a still image of the room, omitting any living thing, and showed the plain picture to whoever was watching. One small room would be easy to manage, but in a huge factory, it would require way too much magic and drain the witch within five minutes.

We discussed strategy for a few more minutes and agreed that Imani would organise everything and call me when things were ready to go. In the meantime, I was going to contact Millicent's dad, Robert, and organise another tattoo cleansing. As positive as all this might turn out to be, we still had to figure out what was going on with Sarah's friend, not to mention the mystery of what had gotten into Ma'am. I hoped she wasn't in some kind of extra trouble to normal. But with Chad and the directors after her blood, that wouldn't surprise me.

Not one little bit.

CHAPTER 8

The next morning, we sat around the PIB conference-room table. Ma'am was at Chad's right, and Chad was at the head, his heels resting on the tabletop. The bulging muscle at Ma'am's jaw jabbed at her poker-face façade. His disrespect even rankled me, and I wasn't a huge fan of the PIB. I helped because I hated unfairness, and it was the right thing to do, but even though Ma'am had tried to recruit me several times, I resisted. Hopefully once we discovered what had happened to my parents, and we got the directors off Ma'am's back, I'd be able to go back to being a professional photographer full-time. No matter how many obstacles plonked themselves in my way, I wouldn't give up the dream.

Chad linked his hands behind his head and rested back into them. Why didn't he just magic a bed next to the table and have a lie-down? Or maybe he'd like to relax in a bubble bath? Imani sat across from me, and we shared an eye-roll. What would we do without that expression? "So, team, we have a new case to look into, I understand. Sarah Blakesley's drugging."

Ma'am answered, "Yes, Sir." She gave no other information, probably wanting to make him work for it.

"What are the facts of the case, and what is your plan, Agent DuPree?"

Ma'am went into school-teacher mode—she spoke to him as if she knew all the answers and was just waiting to catch him out on a mistake. "After her brother got a call that Ms. Blakesley was found unconscious on a Spanish island when she should have been in Paris, he hurried to collect her. Blood tests showed Rohypnol in her system."

"I understand she's a model?"

"Yes, Sir."

"Was it possible she just partied too hard, and we're taking this more seriously than it deserves?" My mouth dropped open, and Will gripped his chair arm. Ma'am blinked forcefully a couple of times. Beren's eyes widened, and he flicked his gaze to Will, no doubt waiting for some kind of explosive reaction. Chad was making way too many enemies. I wondered how many people at the New York office hated him too.

James cleared his throat. "Sarah Blakesley is a professional. She isn't known to miss jobs or take drugs. She stayed at her parents' the night before it happened and didn't leave their house till about six in the morning. Unless there was a silent breakfast or lunch party near where she was found, she did not do this to herself. We've put a call in to the local police, and they had no reports of undue noise in the vicinity that day."

Chad looked at his watch. "I have a breakfast meeting soon, so let's hurry this up. What's your plan? And be aware that we don't have many resources to put into this." Oh. My.

God. This guy was unbelievable. Could he not read everyone's body language? The tense jaws, frowns, eerie stillness.

Ma'am unlocked her jaw. "Don't worry. I'm only putting two agents on this for now: Blakesley and Jawara. Olivia will assist with communication and additional research. I thought it best to include everyone in this room in case this investigation crosses over into the jewellery heist."

Chad wrinkled his brow, slid his legs off the table, and sat up. "Why would you think the two cases are linked?" Was he really that stupid, or was he trying to be difficult?

Ma'am smirked, although he probably read that as friendly. "Just a hunch I have."

"Well, don't go spending PIB dollars on any hunches. I have to answer to the directors, you know."

A serene smile absorbed Ma'am's smirk. "Oh, I won't spend any of our *dollars*. I promise." I stifled a snort. Chad's slip of the tongue had given Ma'am all the moral wiggle room she needed, even though if he complained later that she'd spent pounds, the directors would probably be cranky. But who cared? We had to deal with what we could now and hope there would be a later.

Chad stood. "Good. Now we have that settled, you can work out the annoying stuff yourselves. There's a bacon-and-egg roll calling my name." He made his doorway and left. Thank God.

Ma'am held up her hand, no doubt to silence the numerous complaints about Chad that were eagerly waiting behind everyone's lips. "I will not waste my precious time discussing how stupid someone is. We've wasted enough time with him already." Her magic vibrated along my scalp, and she created a bubble of silence. I was proud of myself for being able to recognise more than a few different spell patterns now.

I hated having to look at the magic with my second sight because people's auras were distracting, but I needed to be able to tell what spell was coming as soon as possible—it wouldn't always be friendly magic, and in a fight, I needed to be prepared.

Ma'am turned her gaze to Beren. "I know I said I was only using Will and Imani for this, but I'd like you to work with Sarah, see if you can help her remember anything. What did you find when you had a look around her head and healed her?"

Beren drew magic, and his laptop appeared on the table in front of him. He opened it and typed something in, then used magic to slide it across the table to Ma'am. "That's the magic signature I found. Someone's definitely tampered with her memory."

Ma'am typed on his laptop. "I'll run it through the database and see what happens." We waited quietly for a couple of minutes. She finally looked up. "Nothing. This is what it looks like."

She magicked the laptop across to Will, and he checked it out, then sent it across to Imani and said, "Okay. I'm thinking we'll go and chat to Sarah, see if there's anything she can remember now she's rested. I also want to go over what she would have done. Even if she can't remember, if we run the scenario by her, she should be able to tell us where she ended up."

Ma'am nodded. "Okay, good idea. Also, I'd like you to take Lily when you investigate. I'm sure her special talent can help us." She looked at Liv, then Millicent. "You two can come with me. There's another case I need help with." She stood and turned her gaze on Will. "Good luck."

He gave a nod. "Thank you, Ma'am. I appreciate you giving me the case."

"There was never any doubt. I'll see you all later." She moved to the door, Millicent and Liv on her heels. I waved to them as they walked past. Seemed we only saw each other when there was work to do. We needed a fun night out, or maybe even a weekend away. Ha, as if that was going to happen anytime soon.

The rest of us stood, made our doorways, and travelled to Angelica's. It was still fairly early, and Sarah wasn't out of bed. After the trauma and Beren's healing, she was exhausted. Will reluctantly woke her—she could always go back to sleep after we'd finished questioning her. While we waited for her to come downstairs, I magicked cappuccinos for Beren, Will, and I, and tea for Sarah and Imani.

I sat next to Will and took a sip of coffee. "Wow, I can't believe Chad is still alive."

Imani chuckled. "I know, right? It's like he was taking the mickey." She shook her head. "I have new respect for Ma'am and her self-control."

"Hey" came a croaky, just-awake voice from the door. I turned. Sarah was in a loose black T-shirt and grey tracksuit pants. You couldn't get less-glamorous attire, but she still managed to look gorgeous, even with dark circles under her eyes and messy hair.

"Sit." I pulled out the chair next to me. Will sat on my other side, at one end of the table.

She shuffled over and sat. "Is this tea?"

"Yep. Just how you like it."

She smiled. "Thanks." She yawned and took a sip.

"Sorry to get you up, love. We'll try to make this as short as possible," said Imani.

"That's okay. I don't remember anything, but from what Will and Beren have told me, we need to figure this out ASAP. I'm really worried about Luisa, not that I remembered she was missing until Will told me." She frowned. "I'm angry at whoever did this. I feel like crap. How dare they take away three weeks of memories."

Will's fierce gaze made me thankful he was on our side. "And it could've been worse. Whoever did this is going to cop it. They've broken witch laws that carry hefty sentences. I won't stop till I catch them."

Sarah smiled. "Thanks. You're the best brother ever. I think I'll keep you." I chuckled. At least she still had her sense of humour. "Whatever you need to ask me, go ahead. I'm as eager as you to figure this out."

"And I'm here to make sure you're healing okay. If you expend too much energy, don't worry. I can help later."

"Thanks, B." Sarah gave a small smile.

Will drank the last of his coffee and magicked his cup away. "Yesterday, you weren't in great shape. Do you remember much of what I told you?"

"Yes, at least I think so. There was a jewellery theft at a fashion show I was in, and my friend Luisa disappeared. Everyone thinks she did it, but I disagreed enough to follow it up. I visited her place, then her friends, and after that, you lost track of where I went." She paused and took a breath. "For what it's worth, I still don't think she'd steal anything. I'm as shocked about it now as I probably was when it first happened."

"Have you ever been to that place in Spain before?"

"No, at least not up until three weeks ago when my memory cuts out. In the last three weeks, I could've been to the moon, and I wouldn't know." She sighed.

I rubbed her back. "If it makes you feel any better, you were really happy and doing well until you disappeared yesterday morning. Nothing spectacular had happened either, so it's not like you're missing much."

She chuckled. "Trust you to think of the positive spin. It just feels like I've been violated, you know?" All I could do was give her my sad face. I hated when I couldn't fix things.

Will continued his questioning. "We do know you were looking for her. If we can replicate your thinking on the day, maybe we'll figure out where you went after you were at her friends' places. Anita apparently told you that Luisa might have been meeting her ex for lunch. How does that sit with you?"

"Not well. Towards the end of their relationship, she was scared of him. He was really controlling, but after they broke up, she said he was pretty much leaving her alone except for the odd message every now and then. I couldn't see her having lunch with him, but then, people do crazy things when they're in love. Not that she still loved him, but she felt sorry for him since she broke it off. And while he was aggressive, she believed he'd never really hurt her." She shook her head.

"Well, let's just assume she had lunch with him, and you believed it. Where would you have gone next?"

"Probably to his place to see if it was true. Even if she wasn't there, I could question him. He'd get a kick out of telling me he'd seen her—he knows I didn't like him much."

"And what if you'd gone there and he hadn't seen her? Where would you go then?"

She shrugged. "She was close to her brother. I suppose I'd go see him."

Imani's phone rang. "Hey, Liv. We're still at Angelica's. What is it?" Imani listened for a while, then her lips made a little O. "Right. Okay. We're onto it. Text me the address so I can find the nearest landing point. Thanks." She hung up, and a piece of paper appeared in her hand. "Ma'am ignored Chad's instructions, as we knew she would, and Liv's uncovered a new lead." She grinned. "On a hunch, Ma'am got Liv to check ownership of the units where you were found. We knew you couldn't have been carried or translocated far. The initial search didn't come up with anyone familiar, but a couple of apartments in the building were owned under company names. And guess who the director of one of them is?"

We waited for her to answer, but it looked like it wasn't a rhetorical question. Being the one with the least patience, I jumped in first. "Okay, I'll bite. Who?"

Imani trained her gaze on Sarah. "Evelyn Taylor, the designer." That didn't surprise me. She obviously had no scruples, the way she'd practically jumped Will in a room full of people.

Sarah's forehead wrinkled, and her mouth opened slightly, as if she were looking for something to say. "I... uh." She shook her head. "I can't believe she would hurt me. I've known her for a few years. She's a bit wild, but she's not the sort of person who would drug me, surely."

"Consider this," Will said. "She couldn't have wiped your mind because she's not a witch. Maybe she's in league with a witch who convinced her that you'd come to no harm. And apart from having three weeks of your memory wiped and feeling unwell for a couple of days, you weren't hurt. I still want to damage the person or persons who did this to you, but in terms of what she would have thought, do you think under those parameters, she'd cooperate?"

Sarah sighed. "Maybe? She's been known to take a drug or two, so she might not think it's anything major. Honestly, after hearing about Luisa stealing the jewellery, and now this, I don't know what to believe anymore." Her shoulders sagged. She looked exhausted, and who would expect anything less? She'd been through so much in the last twenty-four hours, it was crazy.

"You know what?" Will said to his sister. "After Beren checks you out, go back to bed. We'll pay Evelyn a visit and see what's what. If she did this, we'll find out who's been helping her. We'll arrest all of them—Evelyn, Luisa, and whichever witch is involved." Will looked at me and my lame attempt at hiding a grin. "You find *whichever witch* funny, don't you." He shook his head.

I gave him a Cheshire-cat grin. "You know me so well."

Imani held up the paper. "These are search warrants for Evelyn's properties: both the London townhouse and the apartment in Spain. If there's anything to find, we'll find it."

Sarah looked at each of us. "Thanks, guys. Let me know if you crack the case."

Will stood and went to her. He bent down and gave her a hug. "I'll call you as soon as I know anything." He straightened. "Now rest. We'll see you later."

We all said our goodbyes, and Imani sent Will and me the coordinates to our destination. As we headed off, I was pretty confident we'd have this wrapped up quickly.

How wrong I was.

CHAPTER 9

Evelyn might have had money problems, but she sure lived in a nice place while she had them. The contemporary three-storey townhouse was in a popular area of North London near a park. Will and Imani stood on the small front porch, while I waited on one of the three steps leading up to it. "What if she's not home?" I asked.

Will turned to look at me. "We break in and search the place. We have a warrant."

"Oh. Okay."

Will rang the doorbell. It took about a minute, but Evelyn answered it. When she saw Will, her eyes lit up. "Hello, Will. What a *pleasure* to see you." She wore a red Japanese-patterned satin bathrobe, her cleavage front and centre. Will managed to keep his eyes on her face.

"This isn't a social call." He pulled out his PIB badge that looked government official but didn't actually say *paranormal* anywhere. "I'm here on behalf of the investigative government agency I work for. These are my colleagues, Agent Jawara and

Lily Bianchi. We'd like to ask you a few questions about the disappearance of Sarah Blakesley. We also have a search warrant." He held it in front of her so she could read it.

When she was done, she looked up, confusion on her face. "I have no idea what you're talking about. I haven't seen Sarah since the fashion show. How long has she been gone for?"

"We'll be asking the questions, Ms. Taylor. I'd like to do this inside, if you don't mind."

"What if I do mind?" She held her arms up on either side of the doorway, blocking the entrance as best she could. The motion also pulled the lapels of her robe further apart, and she flashed a nipple.

For goodness' sake, could she put some clothes on? Will's ears burnt red. She was gazing into his eyes, defiant and attempting to be alluring. I stepped onto the porch and jammed myself in between Will and Imani. They had nowhere much to go, so we were squished together like people trying to get off a peak-hour train. "Your nipple isn't going to stop us coming in. Honestly, have some pride. Put some clothes on."

Her predatory smile matched her sultry tone. "Oh, but I'm quite proud of my nipples. I'd be happy to show you both of them."

"I bet you would, but save it for the other crims in jail. You can flash your nipples to them as much as you like. We don't have time for that crap. And just so you know, there's a hair growing out of it." There wasn't, but her horrified expression was worth the lie. She yanked the robe together and put her girls away. Thank God.

"Now, are you going to move aside, or am I going to have to move you?" She was way taller than me, but I must have looked as if I meant business because she stepped out of the way and gave us room to get past. The first doorway on the right was open and revealed a living area, so I walked into there and waited for everyone to join me.

Once we were all in the living area, Will turned to Imani. "Can you start the search? Take Lily with you."

"Oh, you want some alone time with me?" Evelyn purred. I looked at her with laser-focussed eyes willing deadly beams to come out. They didn't. Maybe I could give her a tiny electric shock with my magic?

"Lily." Imani's tone said she knew I was contemplating mischief. I quickly whispered a spell and gave Evelyn one last glare before turning and following Imani into the hallway. Imani cocked her head to the side. "What did you just do?"

"Nothing… much. Just a precaution." She gave me an "I can't take you anywhere" look. I shrugged. "A witch has to do what a witch has to do." I smiled sweetly.

"I give up." She turned and led the way from room to room. Imani swept over everything with her other sight looking for magic signatures or spells, and I wielded my camera, looking for any evidence of Luisa, the jewellery, or Sarah.

Once we'd completed the downstairs area, we came back to the first hallway to take the stairs to level two. A pained squeal came from the lounge room. "Ha! That'll teach her." I couldn't help smiling, even though I knew it made me a not-very-nice person.

"What did you do?" Imani's eyes were wide.

"I made a spell that if she touches Will, she gets an electric shock."

Imani snorted, trying to hold back her laugh. "Remind me never to get on your bad side. Anyway, come on; let's get this done."

"Well, I obviously don't want her touching him because it upsets me, but she made him feel uncomfortable at the fashion show. She was all over him, and he didn't like it. At least he said he didn't, and I could see he was uncomfortable. If it was the other way around, a man pawing a woman, you'd probably think I'd done the right thing."

"All right. I concede you have a point. Now, as much as I'd love to stand here and chat, we have work to do."

We covered every square centimetre but found nothing. Hmm, either she was really clever, or nothing happened here. Maybe it all happened at her other property. We returned downstairs. As we entered the room, Evelyn was cradling her hand between her body and other arm. Will gave me his crankypants stare. I smiled and pretended I didn't know what happened—she must have tried to touch him at least one more time. Served her right. I released the spell.

Imani stood next to Will. "Can I have a word?"

"Of course." He looked at me. "You can come too." Ha, he didn't trust me. It was deserved, but I wouldn't do anything to her as long as she kept her hands to herself, and even then, a tiny shock never hurt anyone… well not too badly.

In the hallway, Imani made a bubble of silence. "We didn't find anything. What did you get out of her?"

"She says she hasn't been feeling well and that she slept the last twenty-four hours. I used my talent to look at the very outer layer of her thoughts, and she believes what she's saying, so I'm thinking she's telling the truth. We need to check out the apartment before I come to any conclusions, but at this stage, we'll have to leave her here, free."

We went back into the living area, and Will spoke to Evelyn. "We have agents going through your Spanish apartment, but at the moment, we're done here. Because this is a continuing investigation and you're a person of interest, you can't leave London for the next forty-eight hours. Is that understood?"

She frowned. "Yes. But I didn't do anything. I like Sarah. And I didn't steal those jewels either. Every one of you come here and question me as if I'm guilty. Going bankrupt is not a crime."

Will gazed around at the opulent surroundings, then back at Evelyn. "You don't look like you're doing it too tough. If we need to ask you more questions, we'll be back." She stood, but Will put his hand up. "That's okay. We'll see ourselves out."

Once out on the footpath and walking back to the toilets so we could travel, Will said, "Lily, that wasn't very nice, shocking her. But thanks. She wouldn't take no for an answer."

"My pleasure. I felt a bit mean, but a girl's gotta do what a girl's gotta do to protect the ones she loves."

Imani smirked. "Oh, and it wouldn't happen to be because the girl is insecure, now, would it?"

"I refuse to answer that on the grounds it might incriminate me. But, hey, if you're going to go after a man in front of his significant other without giving two hoots, I can't be responsible for what happens."

Within a few minutes, we were back in Spain catching a taxi from the cathedral. This time, when we buzzed the building intercom, a young man answered. He was tanned, had sandy blond hair, and spoke to us in Spanish. Will said something haltingly, which I took to mean "I don't speak Spanish."

"Ah, not a problem. I'm Antonio. How can I help you?"

"We were here the other day, picking up the woman who was found unconscious by the pool. We have a warrant to search one of the apartments here." Will pulled out the papers and handed them to Antonio. The one problem was that we hadn't gotten Spanish legal papers done. Would British ones still have jurisdiction?

Imani's magic tingled over my scalp, and Antonio handed the papers back to Will without finishing reading them. "Please come in. I'll show you up, but first, I need to collect the key. Please wait by the lift." It probably wasn't right of Imani to cheat like that, but it was for a good cause. If she could look the other way when I electrocuted people, I could look the other way when she *persuaded* them.

Antonio soon returned and took us up to the third floor, letting us into a large apartment that had cream-coloured tiled floors, and pale-yellow walls. "I'll leave you to it. Once you are done, just lock it like this." He demonstrated how the lock worked.

"Thank you very much," said Will.

The door shut behind the concierge, and I went straight to the balcony doors, opened them, and checked out the view, the cool sea breeze feathering my face. The unit overlooked the pool area and ocean—so much gorgeous blue. If someone had moved Sarah from here to the pool, they would have had a good view of us picking her up. I hoped they hadn't stuck around. Surely they would have had no idea about who her family was… except Evelyn knew Will was her brother, but she couldn't have known he'd pick her up so quickly, or even that he would get her rather than an ambulance or police.

Will joined me. "Can you take some photos inside?"

"I sure can." I went back in and stood in one corner so I could see most of the living area and open-plan kitchen. "Show me Sarah here in the last thirty hours." That should cover all the time she went missing with not much extra for mistakes.

I sucked in a breath. There she was, flopped over a man's shoulder. Her torso and arms hung down his back and past his bottom. She was clearly unconscious. I walked closer and took some photos, bending down so I could photograph her face. Yep, her eyes were closed. I walked around the front of him and took shots of his face. He wasn't anyone I'd ever seen before. Longish dark-brown fringe with clipper-cut back and sides. His black, close-fitting shirt looked designer, as did his ripped jeans.

After taking all the pictures I needed, I turned and stood at the balcony door facing outside. "Show me Sarah here in the last thirty hours." Yep, just as I thought. She was still hanging over his shoulder as he stared down at the pool area. *Click. Click. Show me the moment Sarah arrives at the pool area.* He was still on the balcony, and Sarah appeared down by the pool. I clicked a couple more shots, then went inside. "Imani!"

She hurried out of another room. "What is it?"

"Not sure if you found any magical signatures anywhere, but try on the balcony. Looks like the man who did this translocated her from here to there."

She joined me and surveyed the balcony. "There is. Good work, Lily."

"Thanks. It's not like you wouldn't have checked here anyway. I just speeded up your process."

"True, but any and all help is appreciated."

Will came to the balcony door. "So, you got something?"

"Here." I handed him my phone, and he scrolled through the photos.

"I picked up a magic signature too. It's the same one from the pool area yesterday."

Will's smile looked rather shark-like. "Looks as if we have

our man. Now to find out who he is and if he's in this with Evelyn."

We went inside, locked both the balcony door and front door, but didn't leave the apartment. It was time to travel home and see if Sarah knew this man. Maybe we were finally getting somewhere.

❧

We found Sarah reading in front of the TV. She looked up. "Did you find anything?"

I handed her my phone with just the picture of the guy's face when he was alone on the balcony—I didn't want to freak her out seeing herself draped over his shoulder. "Do you know who this is?"

She sucked in a breath. "That's Luisa's ex, Lorenzo Rossi." Had Luisa put him up to it? But then again, she supposedly didn't know he was a witch. Maybe she asked him to just get rid of her but didn't realise how he would.

This had to be hard on Sarah—she was probably coming to the same conclusion I was. "Don't freak out, but scroll across, and you'll see him carrying you."

She did. "That scumbag! I can't believe this. Do you know if he really is working with Luisa or Evelyn?" A note of hope held in her voice, hope that we wouldn't say Luisa.

Will spoke calmly and gently took the phone from her and passed it back to me. "We don't know. We found no evidence at Evelyn's London place, nor at Luisa's place. It's time to check out his house. We have his address from yesterday, but we'll need another search warrant."

Will called Liv, told her what was going on, and what we needed, then hung up. Within five minutes, she had gotten someone at the PIB to magic him the document. "Gee, that was quick," I said. "Doesn't that stuff have to go through a judge?"

Will folded the document and slid it into his inside jacket pocket. "It does. We have a witch judge on call at all times. They're quick, and we had ample proof that we needed this, so there wasn't any convincing to do." Will turned to Imani and me. "Here are the coordinates for the closest landing spot. I'll see you there in a minute."

The golden numbers appeared in my head, so I stuck them on my door. "Bye, Sarah. We'll be back soon." She gave a half-hearted wave, and I stepped through. Another day, another public toilet. At least I hadn't popped in on another unsuspecting person like the time there was an old lady already occupying the cubicle, and she hadn't just magicked herself in there….

I hurried out to give Imani room; then we both ducked outside. We appeared to be in the foyer of an old office building that contained the ghosts of wealth past. Yellow-tinged marble tiles rested on the floor, and an ornate plaster archway framed the front doors. As soon as Will exited another door and joined us, we made our way outside to a busy street, small cars and Vespas droning past, with the occasional high-pitched beep.

Will used his mobile phone to navigate. The brisk ten-minute walk had me sweating under my layers, even though it was a cool day. If only I could have magicked my coat back home without causing a panic.

Luisa's boyfriend lived in a four-storey apartment building opposite a small park. Will buzzed the intercom—there was going to be no stealth about this. I tried not to think about the fact he could make a doorway and leave when he realised who we were. But the point was moot because no one answered the intercom. After Will buzzed again to no response, he magicked the door open, and we went up the stairs to the first floor.

Will knocked, just in case, but nothing happened. He pulled his gun and magicked the door open. Imani took her gun out and followed. I stayed on alert for magic while in the hallway, waiting for them to give me the okay. If someone I didn't recognise was channelling magic, I could warn them. I also made sure my return to sender was up.

About a minute later, Will returned. "It's all clear. You can come in and do your thing."

The small entry foyer had two doorways leading from it. I opened the door to the left. Oh, a closet. The doorway in front of me was open and led into the living area, a large space furnished with contemporary designer pieces—lots of dark leather, glass, and stainless steel. It all looked pretty new. "This stuff must have cost a fortune." Will, who had turned to leave the room, stopped. He spun back around and stared at the furniture. His brow furrowed. "What's wrong?"

"You found an expensive furniture purchase on Luisa's credit card statement that didn't correlate to what's in her apartment. What's the bet that one of these couches is it?"

"You could be right. But it doesn't make sense, unless he stole it from her place. She didn't like him. Why would you buy furniture for someone you broke up with?"

"Unless she just wanted everyone to think she'd broken up with him."

I scrunched my face. "That doesn't make sense. Why would you bother?"

He shrugged. "She'd already told her friends and family that he was controlling. Maybe she was embarrassed and didn't want the grief from everyone?"

I made a noncommittal grunt. That was a possibility, but it didn't add up. "First we need to confirm it's the furniture, and, also, I need to take some photos. Maybe then we'll have a clearer picture."

Will pulled his phone out. "I'm going to google that brand. What was it again?"

"Cassina. I'll check his closet for Gucci stuff. That was another one of the big purchases." The first room I looked in was set up as a gym and had no closets. The next door I entered had a king-size bed with swanky blue-and-white covers. Imani was already looking in the wardrobe. "While you're in there, check for anything new from Gucci."

She answered without turning. "Okay. Come help."

I crouched next to her and scrutinised the shoes, well shoe boxes. He really looked after his clothes. There were so many boxes. I opened them one by one to find, among other things, that none of them were women's shoes. Which meant Luisa wasn't living here. Wherever she'd disappeared to, it wasn't here. Out of the myriad of shoes, I found three pairs of Gucci loafers—two black leather and one of teal-green velvet with the logo embroidered on it in gold. They looked like slippers. Why would anyone wear these outside? Maybe when you could buy expensive things, it was more to show off than to look good. That was the only explanation I could come up with. The more you stood out, the easier it would be for people to know you were wearing a fancy brand. "These are in pretty good condition. I'm not even sure they've been worn yet." I grabbed my phone out of my pocket and searched them up on the net with the model numbers on the side of the boxes. My mouth fell open. "Oh, wow. These shoes are ridiculously expensive."

"Yeah, it's Gucci, love."

"But five-hundred pounds or more?" That was about a thousand Aussie dollars. The things I could do with three thousand dollars. "I wonder what he does for a job?"

Will appeared at the door. "I'd like to know too. That couch in there is the one from Cassina."

"Found a Gucci blazer." Imani had peeled back a jacket cover to reveal a light-brown woollen blazer with pale-yellow Gs all over it.

I went back to Google and checked the price. "Holy mother of a hungry goat! That's over two thousand pounds."

Will got on his phone and made a call. "Hey, Liv. Yes... Can I get everything on Lorenzo Rossi? Yeah, the same guy we got the warrant for." He said it was super urgent, then hung up.

While we waited for that, Imani and Will checked out the rest of the apartment for any clues, and I switched my phone to camera mode. I started in the living room. "Show me the last time Evelyn was here." Nothing. "Show me the last time Luisa was here." Oh, that was another story. My pulse rate kicked up. Even though I didn't know Luisa, my heart went out to her.

It must have been night-time because the lights were on and the interior of the apartment reflected in the windows. Blackness was outside, with sprinklings of lights in the distance. Luisa was lying on the floor on her side, her hands tied behind her back and a gag in her mouth. She was doing her best to look up at Lorenzo. On closer inspection, there were tears on her cheeks and fear in her eyes. And that wasn't the scary part.

She was see-through.

Had he already killed her, or was he going to? Could we still stop it? From experience, we might be able to revive her if we got to her in time, but I didn't think we could stop it from happening in the first place. I took some photos, then focussed on what was in his hand.

The stolen jewellery. A necklace, bracelet, and maybe a couple of pairs of earrings, but it was hard to tell, as they were all gathered together in his palms. The diamonds glimmered in the lamplight—beauty in the hands of a monster. *Click, click, click.* The question now was, had she helped him get away with this and then been turned on, or had he somehow coerced her?

More importantly, where was she now?

Sarah was not going to like this. "Will, Imani," I called out. They hurried into the room. "Check this out." I handed the phone to Will, and they both watched the screen as he flicked through the images. "I asked for evidence of Evelyn being here, but nothing showed up, which means she's never been here before."

"Oh, wow. That girl's in big trouble." Imani looked up at Will. "And Sarah's going to hit you with a big, fat 'I told you so.'"

"I'm a big boy. I can take it. We do what we have with what we have, and we weren't to know. If we were psychic, everything would be so much easier."

"What now?" I asked. "We still might be able to save her." I spoke the words, but hope was dead in my chest. Where the hell would we even start to look? He could have magicked her anywhere in world, or, at least, anywhere in Europe. Another thought hit me—he could have easily killed Sarah. I took a deep, shuddering breath. Thank God he hadn't.

Will's glum face didn't inspire confidence. "We need to go back and see Sarah. She'll know something about his habits. I'll get her to text Lavender as well. He knew her just as well."

Something I could help with. "I have his number. We exchanged them because we were going to stay in touch after everything was fixed. He's a lovely guy." I typed out a text for him to meet us at Angelica's and pressed Send. "Done."

"Right. Time to get back." Will made his doorway and left, Imani and I trailing.

After returning home, we waited five minutes for Lavender to show up; then we grabbed Sarah and sat in the living room on the trusty Chesterfields. Those couches had seen a lot of action since I'd been in the UK, and not the sexy type. We'd had countless unofficial meetings here—it was a lot more comfortable and cosier than the PIB conference room.

When Sarah saw Lavender, her eyes lit up. "Lavvie!" She gave him a huge hug.

"Sweetie, I've been so worried. I wanted to come see you as soon as Lily texted me last night that you were okay, but I knew you needed your rest."

"How did the show go?"

"It went well, but it wasn't the same without you. And you should see the absolute cow they replaced you with. As gorgeous as they come, but a total witch, and not in the magical sense. You better not miss any more jobs, missy."

"I can assure you that I'll do my best not to. The last few days have been horrible." Sarah and Lavender held hands and sat. Imani and I sat opposite them, and Will sat next to his sister—she was going to need all the moral support she could get, and, so too, Lavender. Was it selfish of me to be glad I didn't have to break the news? Reason one hundred and seventy-one that I was a terrible person.

Sarah turned to Will. "So why are we all here?" She probably meant why had we included Lavender.

Will licked his bottom lip. "So, we got into Lorenzo's pl—"

His phone rang. He scowled and slid it out of his pocket. "Hello, Liv. Did you find what I asked for? …great, thanks." He hung up, and his phone dinged with an email. He ignored it and put his phone on the table and faced Sarah again.

"So, you got into Lorenzo's place. Then what?" She looked at him, hope in her eyes. Lavender was staring at Will too. Tears pricked my eyes. What were they going to do when they found out? Gah, this wasn't good. In fact, it was beyond awful.

Will took a breath. "We found items that we believe Luisa bought for him since their break-up."

Lavender piped up, "The Gucci stuff and the Cassina?"

Will nodded. "That's not all. There was no trace of him, but we… we ah—"

I jumped in. "We found some blood, and we think it's Luisa's." I stared at Will. "Will magicked it off to the lab for them to run some tests." We couldn't tell Lavender about my talent, and Will had obviously not thought that through before he decided to include him in this.

Sarah and Lavender both sucked in shocked breaths. Sarah wiped the back of her hand across one eye. "Are you saying she could be dead?"

Will put his arm around her. "Yes. I'm sorry."

"But how can you be sure?" She looked at me, likely realising the unspoken.

My voice was soft. "We're not a hundred percent sure, but as sure as we can be. I'm still holding out hope, as slim as that chance is."

Her face crumpled into grief, and she and Lavender turned to each other and hugged. I shared a despairing look with Will. If only my magic was wrong more often.

Will cleared his throat. "Sarah, I know what we've just told you, and we're fairly sure, but we still need to find her. There is a possibility, albeit a tiny one, that we can save her. You just never know. That's why we came here—not just to tell you both this but to ask where you think he could have taken her. Did they have any special places they liked to hang out, or did he have a holiday house or something?"

"Ah, Will," Imani said gently. "You asked Liv for that information, and you probably have it sitting in your email. Maybe that will give us a clue. In any case, I'd like to look through those documents." At least Imani was on the ball. Will and I were too worried about Sarah. I hoped what Will had just said didn't give her false hope.

"Okay." Will grabbed his phone, opened it, and drew on his magic. His lips moved silently and then a few A4 sheets of paper appeared on the table. "If you want to read that while I talk to these guys, that would be great."

"I'd be happy to." Imani picked up the papers and read.

Will, Sarah, and Lavender chatted quietly. I had nothing to do, so I half listened to them and watched Imani's face become more and more incredulous until I couldn't stop myself. "What is it?"

She jerked her head around to look at me. "He was broke."

"What? But I thought he'd bought lots of expensive stuff for Luisa while they dated?"

Sarah stopped talking and turned to Imani. "He did. He had some high-flying banking job, supposedly."

"Well, according to this"—Imani held up the papers—"he was in debt to the tune of over three hundred and fifty thousand euros. His furniture was repossessed a few months ago. That must be why he got Luisa to buy him new furniture."

I looked at Sarah. "Do you think she felt sorry for him?"

She shook her head. "She didn't mention it, and I doubt it.

There's no way she'd spend crazy money on designer stuff. If she felt guilty or like she owed him anything, she would have bought normal, cheapish furniture."

"The plot thickens," said Lavender.

It sure did. But where the hell had he taken Luisa? I could imagine her lying somewhere scared, waiting for someone to come save her.

But if my photo was anything to go by, we were going to be too late.

CHAPTER 10

After finding out everything we could from Sarah and Lavender, it was decided we'd revisit Luisa's two girlfriends in Florence. They'd spent more time with her, and apparently one of them had been the one to introduce Luisa and Lorenzo. Instead of sending Lavender back, we were doing this one ourselves.

We'd visited the first woman, Sienna, who had nothing to add. She was helpful and let us in to have a quick look around. We found nothing, even with my talent. Now we stood outside her other friend Maria's apartment building. Will buzzed the intercom, and a woman answered, although she sounded older than I expected, and she didn't speak English. Luckily Sarah had agreed to come with us, and she was fluent in Italian. After a bit of convincing, the latch for the front security door clicked, and we went inside.

A short, plump, grey-haired woman wearing an apron over her dress answered the door. She narrowed her eyes as she took in the four of us. Sarah was quick to speak, and I figured she was explaining why we were here. When the old lady looked at me, I smiled, hoping to appear as non-threatening as possible. If worse came to worse, Will could cast a spell on her to make her more agreeable, but that was technically against the rules, and only used in dire times. Although with Luisa missing and in grave danger, I was pretty sure that met the criteria.

Sarah and the woman had a long conversation in which I distinctly heard the phrase "Lorenzo e Maria," which I reckoned meant Lorenzo and Maria. Lorenzo and Maria what? Sarah repeated the names and said something else. The woman said, Lorenzo Rossi. My eyes widened.

Sarah turned to us, her brows drawn together. "She said Maria left yesterday, shortly after a visitor came—which I'm thinking was Lavender. Maria told her grandmother that she was going on holiday with her boyfriend, who just happens to be Lorenzo."

Will scowled. "She must have warned him that Lavender was looking for Sarah. Great, so now they're on the run."

"It would appear so," said Imani. "Does she know where they went?"

Sarah shook her head. Will pressed his lips together. "If we get her mobile number and call her, we can send a tracking spell to her phone… if she answers, that is. Can you get it from her grandmother?"

Sarah turned back to the woman. After a short conversation, the woman motioned for us to stay put. She left and returned a short time later with a piece of paper. Thank God for that. Now, hopefully, Maria would answer her phone.

We thanked Maria's grandmother and left. On the footpath, we stood out of the way of passing pedestrians, and Will punched the numbers into his phone. Before he pressed the dial button, he conjured a spell, ready to release if she answered. "If this doesn't work, we'll have to track her through her IMEI number, but that will mean a call to headquarters and hacking into her phone provider's systems to see where she was last time her phone checked in with a tower. It'll slow us down, and it's not as accurate, but it's better than nothing." At least we had a back-up plan.

I crossed my fingers as the phone dialled. Will held the phone to his ear. Sarah folded her arms, and I bit my fingernail. *Please pick up, Maria.* Then Will answered, and his magic cascaded down my scalp. The spell was free. "Hello, yes, I'd like to order a pizza, thanks."

I heard a muffled voice and then nothing. Will lowered the phone and shrugged. "She thought I was a prank call and hung up. We have what we need." He smiled briefly before resettling his serious face. "Sarah, it's time for you to go home. I don't want you with us for obvious reasons."

She looked as if she might argue, but then the reality hit her—no one wanted to see a dead body, especially not if it was a friend. Okay, so some people might want to see a dead body, but that was just weird. "Thanks, Will. Let me know as soon as you have something."

"I will."

We made our way to the toilets—which was fast becoming the story of my life. Sarah came with us that far before travelling home. Will sent me the coordinates for our next landing spot, and we were off.

At the other end, a large, white-tiled bathroom greeted us. Imani and I hurried out into an airport. Okay, that was different. We found Will. "Where are we?" I asked.

"Bologna Airport."

"And where does the tracking say Maria is now?"

Will looked at the app on his phone. "Same as before. A town called Malacappa. It's about fifteen to twenty minutes' drive. Come on. We'll grab a taxi."

Most of the drive was through farmland. It looked peaceful, but not somewhere you'd holiday. Had she lied to her grandmother, or had Lorenzo lied to her? And what of Luisa? A sickly feeling of helplessness lodged in my throat. The closer we got to our destination, the worse I felt.

A phone rang with a tone I didn't recognise. Imani slid it out of her pocket. "Hello, Amanda Howard speaking." Who? "Ah, yes. Why, thank you. I really appreciate it. Our readers are going to love this interview. Yes. I've put it in my appointment book. My photographer and I will see you then. Thank you. Bye." She hung up and looked at me. "Our interview with that politician is set down for tomorrow afternoon."

"Wow, you work quickly… Amanda."

She smiled. "You betcha. The sooner we get this interview done, the better."

"You can say that again." While I was nervous because we were practically going into the lion's den, so to speak, if we pulled this off, we'd have some valuable information that would lead us closer to RP and all the answers I so desperately sought.

Will checked his phone, then asked the driver to stop. I looked around. There wasn't much here. We'd passed a smattering of houses but nothing that could be called a town or village. Will paid, and we got out. The taxi drove off, leaving us standing in front of a long dirt driveway, in bright sunlight. My skin prickled with vulnerability. "Maybe we should do this at night? We're sitting ducks if he sees us." He was a witch, so our no-notice spells wouldn't work.

"That's why Agent Jawara is going to put on her no-notice

spell, change into some farmer's clothes, and drop her spell. She can be a neighbour coming to borrow sugar. She'll have to be quick with the cuffs. Once they're on, you and I can go in, question him, and look for Luisa. Well, Imani and I will question him." He gave me a sympathetic look. "You'll have to look for Luisa, maybe using your talent. Hopefully this is where he brought her."

I took a deep breath and let it out again. "Okay."

For added secrecy, Imani found a shrub to stand behind while she changed clothes. Her headscarf, faded blue dress, and apron looked the real deal, at least how I imagined an Italian farmer woman to look. I'd actually never seen one except for on TV.

Following his app, Will led us about twenty metres down the road, where he stopped just before we reached the next driveway. A tall stone fence backed by a barrier of closely spaced cypress trees screened the property from the road, and therefore us, from whoever was on the other side.

I looked at Imani. "How are we going to know you're inside?" That was a pretty important question, and I was too nervous to wait for Will to ask.

"I can't exactly use magic—we don't want him to figure this out until it's too late. Even if he can see I'm a witch, there would be no reason for me to use magic at his house. Hang on." Imani got her phone out and set up a text, then put it back in her huge floppy pocket on the side of her dress. "I'll send that once I'm in. I'll just have to press the button."

"Have you got your gun?" Will asked. She nodded, turned, and disappeared behind the fence and greenery. I stepped up to the fence. "Do you think I could climb up and peek, see where the house is?"

"No."

"But don't we need to know where the house is? What if it's two hundred metres up the hill?"

"Then it's two hundred metres up the hill. We'll run." I frowned. I didn't like going in blind. "Trust me, Lily. I know what I'm doing." Yeah, yeah, I knew he knew what he was doing, but it didn't make me feel any better. I wandered up and down the pebbly ground in front of the fence while we waited. Was she in the house yet and couldn't send the message? Was there even good phone reception here? I snatched my phone out of my pocket. It oscillated between one and two bars. Crap.

Will stood next to the stone-wall fence, leaned his back against it, and folded his arms, casual as you please. "How are you not stressing?"

"This is my job. Been there done that hundreds of times. Imani's a good agent. She'll be fine. It's not like we're walking into a den of bad guys." But what if we were? What if he wasn't acting alone? He cocked his head to the side. "Lily, it's fine. Please don't stress." His phone dinged, and a whoosh of air left my body. Thank God. "Time to move. Stay behind me. We're going to go straight in—we're not waiting for them to answer the door this time."

As soon as we reached the driveway, Will pulled his gun out and left it pointed at the ground as he jogged up the hill towards a two-storey, stone home. I donned my return to sender and stayed behind him. All the timber shutters were closed. Maybe they wouldn't see us coming after all.

We reached the front door. Imani's magic grazed my scalp; so too did a different magic.... My eyes widened. I hiss-whispered, "Will, he's in there drawing magic. It's the same magic I felt at the fashion show. Hurry!" It was the efficient, cold power I'd experienced that night just before the jewels went missing. After creating the carnage he left behind, he must've made a doorway and taken Luisa, who was holding the jewellery. That was the only way the photo I'd taken made sense.

Will dropped all attempts at stealth and magicked the door open. It slammed inwards and crashed against the wall. He held his gun in front and rushed inside. I drew from the river of power, ready for anything, and followed.

Beyond the entry was a living room. In the middle of the room, Imani and Lorenzo stood and maintained return-to-sender spells. A shiny black rope was around his torso, pinning his arms to his sides. I had no idea what it did, other than tie him up. She must have managed that before he realised what was going on. It didn't stop him spewing magic her way though. A spark bounced off her invisible shield and hit his. A brunette with long wavy hair stood just out of the way staring at them, blinking. It wasn't Luisa, so it must've been Maria. She was obviously wondering what the hell was going on.

Will hurried over, gun pointed at Lorenzo. "Stop drawing your magic. You're under arrest." As Will leaned over, one hand reaching for Lorenzo's wrist, the witch stepped out of the way. Great. He didn't know when he was outgunned.

Finally gathering her wits, Maria took one look at Lorenzo and ran into another room—wise woman. I didn't think we'd have to worry about her for now. She wasn't a witch, and we could easily track her down later if we had to. The danger was in front of us.

Imani walked around to the other side of Lorenzo, and she and Will approached him from two directions. I was blocking his route to the door—not that I looked like I'd give much resistance, but there was no way I was letting him past. His gaze flicked between Will and Imani. He'd already dismissed me, but to be fair, I wasn't pointing a gun at him.

Will took a step closer to Lorenzo. "Drop the magic now, or I'll shoot."

Lorenzo laughed. "I have a shield." He stepped backwards again, heading for a doorway next to the one Maria had run out of.

"Where's Luisa?" Imani asked.

His smirk was pure evil. "I don't know. Why do you ask?"

Maria returned. She wasn't as scared as I thought she was. I furrowed my brow. Why was her hand behind her back? What was she hiding? She jumped towards Will, her hand flinging out from behind her. The kitchen knife she held jabbed straight for Will's back. "No!" Without thinking, I shot magic her way. Just as the tip of the blade connected with Will's skin, a bolt of lightning speared her. She screamed and dropped to the floor, smoke rising from her skin and clothes. Her blackened hair and skin meant she probably wasn't getting up again. Oops. Add another one to my body count. I had but a moment to feel remorse before Lorenzo, murder in his eyes, launched himself at Will.

Imani shot Lorenzo in the leg. He fell, still tied up, and smashed his face into the stone floor. Imani jumped on him and cuffed both hands behind his back, then the black rope disappeared.

"What was that?" I asked.

She turned her head to look at me. "Something to stop him making a doorway. An anti-leave spell. He was bound to this place with my magic."

"Oh, cool."

Lorenzo groaned, and Will rubbed his lower back where the knife had connected. His hand came away with a smudge of blood, but it didn't look serious, thank God. He looked at me. "Thank you."

"Always. I think you owe me one now."

He grinned. "I think you're right."

Maria lay dead in a singed heap. Her poor grandmother. What had I done? Why hadn't I had a plan for what I would do? Imani, finished with Lorenzo, stood and placed an exasperated gaze on me. "Lily, you've just killed a witness. We could've used her later. You really need to finesse your magic. You can't go around killing people all the time. You're going to get in trouble one day. Remember that you should only use reasonable force."

"She was about to plunge a knife into Will. I didn't have time to think, and you're right: I didn't have a plan. I know it was stupid. I'm sorry." My shoulders sagged.

"Well, you'll need to push that to the side for now, love. We need to find Luisa. Will can take Lorenzo back to headquarters and send the forensics team in while we search for her."

Will looked at Lorenzo and then the body before looking up at me. "Are you sure you'll be okay?"

"Yep. Imani knows what she's doing, and we need my photographic skills. I'll take some photos so we have a clearer picture of what happened."

"Okay. Be careful." He grabbed Lorenzo and pulled him up to stand. Will created a doorway, then pushed him through.

Imani and I searched the ground floor, but there was nothing. We both headed upstairs. Unfortunately, we found what we were looking for in the second bedroom we looked in. Luisa, still tied up as she'd been in my photo, lay on the floor, her face waxen. Imani checked for a pulse. "Oh, goodness, she's freezing. The poor girl."

My magic was right again. Damn. We'd warned Sarah of

this outcome, but the confirmation of it would still be devastating for her and Lavender. Now we had to prove who was behind it. If Luisa had been innocent, her name should be cleared. Her family had enough to deal with.

I slid my phone out of my pocket and switched it to camera mode. "Show me who was behind the theft of the jewels." I turned in a slow circle, and there he was—Lorenzo sitting on the bed, staring at the wall. He was alone. I took a pic and lowered the phone.

"Verdict?" Imani asked.

"It was all him. Does that mean he either blackmailed Luisa or controlled her with magic?"

"Looks that way, love. We'll know more once they've done an autopsy. They'll be able to see any spells that altered her mind, as long as they look in the next few days." Magic signatures fading was a real problem for law enforcement. "Let's go back downstairs and wait where we won't disturb any evidence. Once the team gets here, we can go back to headquarters."

We trudged down to the kitchen and sat at a small table to wait. I shuddered. There were two bodies nearby that were waiting for justice. I just hoped we could give it to them.

CHAPTER 11

Two days later, we all sat around the PIB conference-room table. Chad was blathering on about how proud he was. While he did that, I tuned out. There was a fair bit still left to do over the next few days. I hadn't called Robert yet for round two of tattoo eradication, and Imani and I were donning disguises and interviewing the MP Graham Clarke this afternoon. My mouth dried. If RP discovered I was there, they could come and disable me with excruciating pain. Damn tattoo.

"And now I'll hand this over to Agent DuPree. She can explain the details of the case." He looked at her and smiled condescendingly. "I wouldn't want to steal your thunder." What the hell? It was more likely that he had no idea what was going on and didn't know how to explain anything. How much longer did we have to put up with this ridiculous excuse for an agent?

Ma'am's smile was genuine as her gaze touched on each person around the table, with the exception of Chad. "I want to thank you all on a job well done. We've broken the case open in record time. Seems our criminal, Lorenzo, was a collector of human girlfriends whom he would sponge off. Some of the autopsy results are back, and both women—Maria and Luisa—had been compelled by magic. Luisa was compelled to buy him expensive things and to take the jewellery, which he quickly sold. We found the cash hidden at his parents' house. She took the jewellery while he entered via a doorway for which he'd previously set up a landing spot. He magicked out the lights, thumped a few people—including Sarah Blakesley—then made another doorway, taking Luisa and the jewellery with him. Maria had been compelled to give him money but also to try and kill Agent Blakesley." Ma'am looked at me. "Thank you for saving his life, Lily. A bit overzealous, but under the circumstances, it can be forgiven. I'm thinking due to the number of cases you find yourself on that some more intense training is in order."

Not getting totally chewed out was an improvement. "Thank you, Ma'am. That would be great." Whatever training they gave me, I'd grab with both hands. I'd killed a woman who shouldn't have even been there and who certainly wouldn't have tried to kill Will if she'd been in her right mind. I'd made a huge mistake. Acidic guilt and sadness corroded my insides. *I'm sorry, Maria.*

Will tapped my arm. When I looked at him, he shook his head. "You saved my life. Don't beat yourself up about it. If we were non-witch law enforcement, you would've had to shoot her dead."

"Yeah, but we're not. If I'd been better prepared, I could've captured her in air, or ropes, or something."

"Those spells are complicated. You wouldn't have had time. Another second and that blade would've been straight through my kidneys. You did the right thing." I gave him a thankful smile.

Ma'am clasped her hands in front of her on the table. "We've cleared Evelyn the designer from any wrongdoing."

I grumbled under my breath. She hadn't exactly been innocent—the way she'd gone after Will. But I supposed I could let that go since she'd had her electric shocks. Was it my imagination, or was I becoming eviler by the day? And what kind of a word was eviler? That sounded weird, like it wasn't really a word. I jerked my head up. Oops, Ma'am was still talking.

"We're clearing Luisa's name, of course, and her family will be notified so they can bury their daughter in peace. We've handed over some information to the insurers so they can chase up who might have bought the jewellery." She flicked an irritated glance at Chad. "Our budget doesn't support further investigation into the matter now that the main crime has been solved."

Chad folded his arms. "Too right it doesn't."

Ma'am raised her brows but said nothing. She was really doing a great job of holding the anger in. Surely she'd explode one day.

Chad stood and looked at Ma'am. "I'm assuming we're done. That sounds like all of it."

She cleared her throat and looked up at him. "Yes. Yes, that's it. We're done." If only we could be done with him forever. I sighed.

"Excellent. I'll see you tomorrow morning for our next case meeting. As for the rest of you agents, well done, and have a good afternoon." He walked out the normal door, everyone watching him. I could imagine what everyone was thinking, but we were good little witches and uttered not a word.

Ma'am looked at Imani and me. "You ladies have somewhere to be this afternoon, I understand."

"Yes, Ma'am," said Imani.

"Best get to it then. You are excused."

"Thanks." I stood, made my doorway, and stepped through to Angelica's reception room, trusting Imani would soon follow. As I unlocked the door and went through to the hallway, Imani arrived.

We got ready in the living room. I magicked on some faded jeans and a hoodie, plus a blonde wig and brown contact lenses. Imani magicked out of her uniform and into a pinstriped blue shirt and pencil skirt. A large black handbag hung over her shoulder. She finished the look with owl-like glasses, make-up, and a straight-haired dark wig. I magicked a camera with a huge flash to myself. We travelled to the Manchester Conference Centre and ordered an Uber to his office, which was five minutes' drive away.

My leg jiggled on the drive over, and I bit my fingernails. What if he recognised me somehow? What if RP had passed my photo around to all members so they knew what I looked like in case they came across me? That made total sense since one or other of them was always trying to kidnap or kill me. I touched my wig, making sure it was on straight.

"Stop fussing, love. It'll be fine. We've got this under control."

"Try telling the walruses in my stomach."

She raised her brows. "Multiple?"

"Yes, multiple. They're wrestling in there."

She chuckled. "Trust me. We'll get what we need and get out of there. Okay?" I nodded and tried to ignore the nausea I had to keep swallowing.

The Uber stopped about twenty metres down from an

office complex. "That must be it." I rubbed my hoodie sleeve where it covered the tattoo. *Please don't find out who I am.* I touched my wig one more time.

Imani had paid and was getting out. "Come on. I need some good photos today." She winked.

I sucked in a breath and hopped out, scanning the surroundings for anyone who looked suspicious. I checked my phone. "We're two minutes early. Can we just stay out here for another minute?"

Hands on hips, she conjured a bubble of silence. "Really? This from the woman who stood on Tower Bridge and brought down a powerful witch only weeks ago? This from a woman who just saved her boyfriend from a knife-wielding zombie? This from a woman who is not afraid to go toe to toe with Angelica?" She cocked her head to the side. "I can spout off some more instances of bravery for you if you're not convinced. And don't forget what I told you many months ago, at the funeral. You're special, Lily, and the witch world will one day rely on you to do something extra special. Believe in yourself; the rest of us do."

I blinked back tears of gratitude. She was going out of her way to make me feel better. "Thanks, Imani. You're an incredible friend. I know I wouldn't have gotten through half of this stuff without you and everyone by my side. I don't think it's me who will save the day, but us as a team. We make an awesome team." I smiled.

She grinned. "That we do. Okay, so are we gonna get this done?"

I straightened my shoulders and pretended fear wasn't humming through my veins. "Yep. Let's do it." We walked towards the three-level, glass-fronted office building. Graham Clarke MP was plastered across the glass façade of a first-floor office. Some of my fear morphed into butterflies. Would we finally get some decent information that would lead to all our questions being answered? This could be the next gigantic step in our investigation.

We were about twenty metres from the building. I took one last look up at where we were going.

A thunderous boom tore from the building.

I was thrown backwards and slammed into the ground, the air forced from my lungs. In seconds, someone landed on top of me as glass shattered on the footpath and concrete peppered the ground. Imani's magic prickled my scalp. "Stay down." It was hard to hear her over the ringing in my ears. What the hell had happened?

A second explosion vibrated the air. Deadly debris clunked and thudded against the invisible shield Imani must have made. I peered up from under her.

Oh, crap.

Where Graham's office had been was a gaping hole. People screamed and moaned. Blood spattered the footpath. Sirens wailed in the distance.

Imani stood and pulled me up. I checked my camera—it seemed to have survived. "Imani, you have blood on your face."

She touched her cheek and winced. "I think there's some glass." She drew on her magic, and a sliver of glass slid free and dropped to the ground. "All good." She gave me the once-over. "You don't look so great either. Your arm is bleeding."

I looked down. So it was, but not much. It could wait for Beren. "I'm okay. It only hurts a little bit."

"Good." I peered around at the carnage, people lying on the ground, steel reinforcement poking out of the concrete where the floor of Graham's office used to be. I stepped towards someone, intending to help. Imani grabbed my good arm. "Sorry, love, but it's time to get to safety. We're not going to get any information from him today. They must have known we were coming."

"What's the bet he was inside." We were never going to get that information. Disappointment soured my tongue. RP had beaten us to it. A shiver sluiced through me.

Imani tugged my arm again. "Come on. It's not safe here." She flicked her gaze around as members of the public crouched in groups to help those who were down.

Had that been a warning, or had we been lucky?

Whatever it was, I didn't want to find out today. I gave her a nod and ran till my breath scoured my throat. All I wanted was to go home. There would be plenty of time to figure this out later… wouldn't there?

❧

Angelica's kitchen had become a makeshift triage. Our wigs sat on the table while Beren fussed over both of us. Once he'd removed three small pieces of glass—two from me and another from Imani—seen to any grazes and bumps, and assessed us for concussion, we were declared healed and fine.

Will, James, and Angelica stood around the table watching everything. Angelica looked at Imani. "I'd like you to write a full report on this. Hand it to James at his place. This doesn't leave the group. The last thing we need is for Chad to get wind of what we're doing."

Imani responded, "Yes, Ma'am."

Will scowled. "How did they know?"

James looked at Imani. "Could they be tracking your phone?"

"I didn't even use a PIB one." She shook her head. "There's no way they could've traced my burner phone back to me."

"Could it have been a coincidence?" I asked. Surely that was one of our options.

Angelica's voice was adamant. "I don't believe in coincidences. I also don't believe we have a traitor in our group. It was either the phone or your tattoo."

I glared at my arm, hating the snake coiled there with all of my being. Millicent's dad had turned off the tracking device, but could they somehow listen into our conversations, even with a bubble of silence protecting them. I couldn't believe it. "Maybe they checked out our made-up credentials and couldn't find anything?"

James folded his arms. "But how did they get from that to killing someone? Well, killing six people, actually. It's being reported as a terror attack at the moment, and I've had one of the police on the ground confirm they believe Graham was in there. It will be a while until they identify the bodies and confirm anything. In the meantime, we wait."

Will nodded. "Agreed. I also think we should leave Lily out of any discussions from now on, at least until her tattoo is removed."

My mouth dropped open. "You can't! Robert's already said they can't spy on me through this."

James pulled out a chair and sat opposite me. "But we don't know for sure. Until we figure out how this leaked, we can't take any chances. I'm sorry, Lily."

How could my life be going from bad to worse? I shut my eyes and counted to ten. Just because I couldn't be part of the discussions didn't mean there would be no discussions. I could trust them to make good decisions. They had my best interests at heart, as I had theirs. I opened my eyes. "Okay. Until we can confirm where we stand, I'll sit out of any discussions."

Angelica's eyes widened, slipping out of the safety of her poker face. "You never cease to amaze me, Lily. I don't want to be part of any discussions either, so I'm going to leave now. Don't update me on anything. I have my hands full at work at the moment. As I said before, I'm trusting this to your capable hands, James." What was going on with her? I shared a concerned brow wrinkle with Will. "I'll see you all later." She made a doorway and left.

"Right. That's my cue to leave. I've got a tonne of paperwork to get through before tomorrow. If you have any aches and pains that need looking at later, let me know." Beren smiled, then left.

"I'd love to stay and chat, but I have to get back too." James came around the table, bent over, and gave me a quick hug. "We'll get to the bottom of this; don't worry." I gave him a "what are ya gonna do?" smile. "I'll call you later." He waved and was gone.

Imani stood and looked at Will. "Time for us to get back to work. Sorry to leave you, love. Will you be okay by yourself?"

I guessed I'd have to be. This afternoon would take some processing, but I wasn't sure if I was ready for that yet. The last three days had been pretty horrible, actually. I gave Will and Imani my best fake smile. "I'll be fine. There's a book on my iPad I've been wanting to read for ages. This afternoon might just be the perfect time. I also need to catch up on *Escape to the Chateau*." One of my recently discovered favourite shows about an English couple who buy and renovate a gorgeous French chateau. I'd put buying a chateau on my to-do list, but the list was so long, I'd probably never get around to it. It was a pleasant dream to have though.

Will smiled. "When this whole thing is over, we'll rent a chateau for a week if you like, get everyone on holiday. What do you think?"

I grinned. "That's the best idea you've had for ages!"

"Nonsense. I have amazing ideas all the time, like this one." He pulled me up, wrapped his arms around me, and kissed the bad afternoon away. Imani cleared her throat and said goodbye. I could only assume she'd made her doorway and left because my eyes were closed, and all I knew was Will.

There were worse ways to end a day, and I should know because I'd lived them. But not today. Today had finished with me in my loved one's arms. There was no better ending than that.

ALSO BY DIONNE LISTER

Paranormal Investigation Bureau

Witchnapped in Westerham #1

Witch Swindled in Westerham #2

Witch Undercover in Westerham #3

Witchslapped in Westerham #4

Witch Silenced in Westerham #5

Killer Witch in Westerham #6

Witch Haunted in Westerham #7

Witch Oracle in Westerham #8

Witchbotched in Westerham #9

Witch Cursed in Westerham #10

Witch Burglar in Westerham #12

Vampire Witch in Westerham #13

Witch War in Westerham #14 (out Nov 2020)

The Circle of Talia

(YA Epic Fantasy)

Shadows of the Realm

A Time of Darkness

Realm of Blood and Fire

The Rose of Nerine

(Epic Fantasy)

Tempering the Rose

ABOUT THE AUTHOR

USA Today bestselling author, Dionne Lister is a Sydneysider with a degree in creative writing and two Siamese cats. Daydreaming has always been her passion, so writing was a natural progression from staring out the window in primary school, and being an author was a dream she held since childhood.

Unfortunately, writing was only a hobby while Dionne worked as a property valuer in Sydney, until her mid-thirties when she returned to study and undertook a creative writing degree. Since then, she has indulged her passion for writing while raising two children with her husband. Her books have attracted praise from Apple Books and have reached #1 on Amazon and Apple Books charts worldwide, frequently occupying top 100 lists in fantasy and mystery. She's excited to add cozy mystery to the list of genres she writes. Magic and danger are always a heady combination.

Made in the USA
Monee, IL
21 September 2020

43124533R00104